I0574892

LAST RESORT

TREASURE TRAIL - BOOK 3

MORGAN BRICE

eBook ISBN: 978-1-64795-073-6
Paperback ISBN: 978-1-64795-074-3
Last Resort, Copyright © 2024 by Gail Z. Martin.
Cover by Lou Harper.

The right of the author to be identified as the author of this work has been asserted in accordance with the Copyright, Designs and Patents Act 1988.

All rights reserved. No part of this book may be reproduced in any form or by any electronic or mechanical means, including information storage and retrieval systems, without written permission from the author, except for the use of brief quotations in a book review.

This is a work of fiction. Any resemblance to actual persons (living or dead), locales, and incidents are either coincidental or used fictitiously. Any trademarks used belong to their owners. No infringement is intended.

NO AI TRAINING: Without in any way limiting the author's exclusive rights under copyright, any use of this publication to "train" generative artificial intelligence (AI) technologies to generate text is expressly prohibited. The author reserves all rights to license uses of this work for generative AI training and development of machine learning language models. No AI was used in the creation of this book.

Darkwind Press is an imprint of DreamSpinner Communications, LLC

MORGAN BRICE

LAST RESORT

ONE

BEN

"This brings back memories." Ben Nolan and his partner carried the last boxes up the stairs. "I spent too many Saturdays in my twenties helping my friends move in and out of apartments for free pizza and beer."

"Look at it as a built-in fitness workout," Erik Mitchell, his boyfriend, replied. "The good thing is that most days, you don't need to go up and down more than once."

"I'm sure I can come up with reasons to stay in." Ben dropped his voice to a sexy growl and gave Erik a knowing look.

Erik shook his head fondly. "Sounds good—but we still need to go to work sometime."

Erik owned Trinkets, the antique shop on the first floor of the old Victorian house where their apartment took up the second level. "Can't beat the commute," he added.

"True—and mine's still totally walkable unless the weather is foul." Ben managed Nolan Resort Real Estate, owned by his aunt and uncle. Until recently, he had stayed in one of the company's rentals. Ben had moved in with Erik a few months ago, but forgot about a stack of boxes that were still stored in Trinkets' back room.

The important stuff had already found a place in the apartment.

Now Ben needed to figure out what in these last boxes to keep or toss. He'd packed long enough ago that he had forgotten what remained.

"Actually, I was surprised how fast I got used to the stairs," Erik told him. "My place in Atlanta had an elevator, but nowhere near the charm."

Both Ben and Erik had recently moved to Cape May, New Jersey, to make a fresh start after their old lives went off the rails. Ben stepped away from being a Newark cop after a betrayal and a near-fatal shooting, and becoming a private investigator had left him burned out and bitter. Erik left his high-profile work stopping art fraud and antiquities smugglers when a bust gone wrong nearly got him killed—and his boyfriend cheated. Differing circumstances led them to Cape May and chance brought them together. Ben thanked his lucky stars every day for how things had turned out.

"Now we just have to figure out what's worth keeping." Ben surveyed the stacks of boxes in the living room. "We already have an *interesting* decorating style."

They had found a quirky way to blend his statues of Spider-Man and Optimus Prime and wall art of some of his favorite comics and sci-fi movies with Erik's more traditional taste, honed by his work for art museums.

"Bring it on," Erik said with a laugh. "It's good to shake things up."

Ben reeled him in for a kiss. "I can think of ways to get a whole lotta shakin' going on," he growled.

Erik returned the kiss and stepped away. "Hold that thought. We need to be able to navigate through the living room, so the boxes can't stay—which means unpacking."

"Spoil sport," Ben grumbled good-naturedly.

Erik ordered hot subs for lunch so they could work without worrying about food, an Italian club for Ben and meatballs for Erik. Ben would have liked to turn up the music while they worked, but the shop downstairs was open, so they kept the volume down.

"Thank Susan for me." Ben polished off the last of his sub and tossed the wrapper in the trash. "I appreciate her handling the store so you can help me."

Erik laughed. "Are you kidding? She would have chased me out if I had tried to stay. She's delighted we're living together and passes along tidbits about keeping relationships 'fresh.'" He grinned. "It's kinda cute."

Susan Hendricks, his next-door neighbor and now part-time shop associate, was widowed after a long and happy marriage and couldn't resist sharing motherly wisdom and casserole recipes.

"We certainly don't want to disappoint her." Ben sidled up to Erik for another kiss. "Let's at least clear a path to the bedroom."

"Unpack first, sex later. How do you want to do this?"

Ben stood with his hands on his hips surveying the stack of boxes. "I'm not even sure I remember what's packed. I think I need to take everything out, decide what to keep, and then we can figure out whether to sell, donate, or pitch everything else."

"Sounds like a plan," Erik replied. "How can I help?"

"Good question. Maybe if you open a box, then I'll go through it while you unload the next one," Ben said.

"Works for me."

Ben couldn't help being nervous. He felt acutely aware of invading Erik's space, even though they had already been living together for weeks.

Ben sat on the floor and began to unpack a box. Erik found a spot across the room and peeled off the tape from another one.

"Oh wow. I forgot I had these." Ben pulled out action figures and Comic-Con souvenirs. In his old apartment, he had a shelf that ran around the top of the room to display his collection.

"Those are pretty cool." Erik looked up. "Where do you want to put them?"

Erik had been generous welcoming Ben into the apartment, but Ben didn't want to overstep. "Let's unpack stuff and then decide. I've lived without these things for quite a while, so this might be a good time to purge." Some of the boxes hadn't been opened since his move from Newark, taken from the back room of his rental unit to the storage room at the store.

"If something's important to you, we'll figure out how to display it," Erik told him. "This is your home now."

Ben felt grateful for Erik's repeated assurances, but old insecurities were difficult to put to rest. He enjoyed seeing the action figures again as he handled them, but had already started thinking of which to keep and which to sell now that he realized some had lost their appeal.

The next two boxes held graphic novels, and Ben knew he wanted to look those over more closely. A third box held tabletop role-playing games that he used to enjoy with a group of friends in Newark but hadn't thought about since his move.

"I'm willing to learn how to play those if you'll teach me." Erik glanced up from the box of paperback books he had opened.

Ben smiled. "That could be fun, something to do when Sean and his friends are in town." His cousin had been Ben's first gaming partner. "Some of these were better than others. I think I can cull a few. Same with those paperbacks." Ben nodded toward the books Erik stacked nearby. "I'm not going to re-read a bunch of those, shouldn't have packed them all."

"Whatever you're worrying about, stop it," Erik said as he cut the packing tape to flatten a box.

"Who says I'm worrying?"

"The little squinch between your eyebrows." Erik gave him the side eye.

At thirty-five and five-foot-ten, Erik was two years older and three inches shorter than Ben, blond and blue-eyed compared to Ben's dark hair and green eyes. Erik's hair fell in a natural wave, while Ben preferred a shorter fade. Together, they seemed to prove that opposites attract.

"I just don't want to take up too much space," Ben admitted. "I love the idea of living together. But now that we're trying to find a place for everything, I'm afraid it'll seem like I'm taking over."

"Was that why you hid your statues in the office at first and didn't put anything in the living room or our bedroom?" Erik raised an eyebrow.

Busted, Ben thought. "Everything looked very pulled together in those rooms. My stuff didn't match."

Erik's background in art and art history, plus his time working for museums, gave him eclectic taste reflected in his choice of prints of famous paintings that spanned from the Renaissance to present day. While Erik shared Ben's love for pop culture and had never disparaged Ben's choice of décor, Ben couldn't help feeling like his taste lacked sophistication.

"Like I said when you moved in—who says anything has to match?" Erik challenged gently. "Our stuff is a reflection of us, and we fit together just fine."

"Mine isn't as classy," Ben admitted.

"You do realize that 'classical' artwork was the pop culture of its time, right?" Erik leaned against the couch. "People just think it's snooty because it's old. And what pop culture lacks in pretention it makes up for in passion. But most of all, it's something that you love, and I love you. There's no need to hide anything. Our home should reflect who we *both* are."

It had taken some convincing, but Ben and Erik had worked together to mesh their favorite things, and now Ben loved the mix of décor that was uniquely them, blending Batman with Basquiat.

Erik set one box aside and started to open another. "I knew what I was asking when I brought up moving in together. We'll figure it out. I didn't like saying goodnight and watching you drive away."

That had happened less and less often the longer we dated, Ben thought. Still, having him give up his rental to move in was a different level of commitment—and risk—than staying overnight, knowing there was somewhere to go back to in the morning.

"I didn't like that part either," Ben confessed. "And I know things will sort themselves out. I want this. I want you. I'm still just a little out of my comfort zone."

Erik opened the next box and then paused with a troubled expression. "Um, maybe you'd better do this one. I'm picking up a strong resonance from some of the pieces." Erik's ability as a psychometric meant he could read the history and emotional resonance of objects by touching them. That wasn't usually an issue with everyday items, but sentimental possessions often packed a wallop.

"Let me see," Ben said, and Erik slid the box to him. One look brought back memories. Old photos of him and his now-estranged mom, stepdad, and half-brothers. A few pictures with former boyfriends or friends he had lost touch with. Commendations from the police department in Newark before he was betrayed by someone on the force. An emotional minefield of things he didn't want to remember and couldn't bear to get rid of.

"You okay?" Erik asked after Ben sorted through the box in silence. "I didn't get happy vibes from whatever's in there."

Ben tried to shake off the memories. "Yeah, I'm fine. This is actually good—I should have gone through this stuff long ago."

"Time helps make decisions." Erik picked a box with more paperbacks. "What's hard to deal with at one point turns out not to be a big deal when you come back later."

It took less time than Ben expected to find a place for his belongings. He'd always prided himself on "traveling light," but confronted with the evidence, Ben wondered if he hadn't kept himself a little too ready to move on.

Not anymore. Maybe someday we'll outgrow this apartment and get a house we don't have to share with the shop, but I'm not going anywhere without Erik.

By the end of the afternoon, they had found shelf space for the books and knickknacks Ben wanted to keep and re-filled several boxes with items he no longer wanted. He glanced at his phone and was surprised to see it was already time for dinner.

"How about pizza?" Erik asked when the last box had been flattened. Ben opened his mouth to agree when a knock at the door startled both men. Thanks to the magical protections that surrounded Trinkets and Erik's apartment, only a handful of trusted people were able to get close.

"Are you finished unpacking yet?" Susan stood outside the door holding a casserole in oven mitts. Her short brown hair hid gray strands, and her trim form—even in her sixties—was a testament to a dedicated Yoga routine. The afternoon had flown, and they were past the shop's closing time.

"I figured you wouldn't feel like cooking after all that work, so I brought my 'famous' chicken tetrazzini." Susan passed the mitts and the dish to Erik. "It's Cole's favorite," she confided about her son, the Cape May chief of police.

"Come on in." Erik moved aside. "The boxes are gone, and we might move some things around, but it's mostly done."

Susan walked into the living room and looked around, then nodded. "I love the mix. It's unique. Now that you've mixed 'his' and 'his,' it'll be interesting to see what you add that you pick out together."

Erik set the casserole in the oven and turned back to their guest. "Thank you for dinner. You saved us from pizza."

"Oh, I love good pizza," Susan said. "But there's nothing like a homemade casserole."

"Can you stay and eat with us?" Erik asked.

Susan shook her head. "Thank you, but I've got my own meal in the oven at home. I did want to bring you this." She took a package out of her large purse and handed it off. "It came in the mail for you at the shop. Anything that's hand-printed on brown paper packaging gets my attention. Definitely not your usual mail order."

Erik reached for the envelope and then recoiled as his fingers touched the paper, letting it fall onto the table. Susan and Ben looked at him with concern.

"What's wrong?" Ben moved protectively to get between Erik and the package.

"Sorry," Erik said, chagrined. "Nothing dangerous—just surprising. Whatever's in there had a strong emotional connection for the sender. Not sure whether it was positive or negative."

"Is it safe to open?" Susan asked.

"It should be," Erik replied. "And I'll use gloves when I handle it."

"Let's see what's inside." Ben got scissors and cut the package open, careful not to damage the address or anything within. "No return address. That's never a good sign unless there's a note."

Six yellowed poker chips tumbled onto the table. Ben lifted one to the light. "Fun Factory, Sewell Point, NJ," he read aloud. "Clay chips, pretty old," he observed.

"Casinos haven't used clay chips since the 1950s," Erik mused. "I've never heard of the Fun Factory."

Susan shook her head. "Neither have I, and I've lived in Cape May all my life."

Erik let his open palm hover above the chips. "I'm picking up excitement, tension, disappointment, and an undercurrent of danger." He let his touch magic read the impressions left by the emotions of the person who owned them.

"There's no ghost present at the moment, but I'm sensing enough energy that I think the chips still might be haunted. Maybe the ghost wants to get to know us better before he or she shows up," Ben said after concentrating for a moment, and Erik nodded. Both men could see ghosts who weren't strong enough to make themselves visible to others.

"I think there's definitely a story behind them." Erik frowned as he stared at the mysterious pieces. "Is there a note?"

Ben dug into the envelope and pulled out a piece of paper. "Take these with my blessing. They've been nothing but trouble," he read aloud. "There's no signature."

"Do you think they're safe?" Susan had worked for Trinkets long enough to have seen haunted, cursed, and possessed objects, which made her definition of "safe" different from what most people meant.

"I'm not picking up anything harmful, although the chips might have somehow caused harm to their owner," Erik said slowly as if he was sorting out the impressions. "Maybe the person was a compulsive gambler and got into debt or trouble with the mob. I'd like to know more about the Fun Factory. From the look of the chips, I'd say they were made before 1920."

"The Jersey Shore was pretty wild back then," Ben said. "Cape May's Mob was a bit more 'refined' than the Atlantic City crowd, but those were the Capone years. I'd be surprised to find a gambling establishment that didn't have Mafia connections."

Here we go again, Ben thought. He'd gotten shot as a cop because he dug up information about old Mob cases people wanted to leave buried. Erik's art fraud investigations had pitted him against Russian oligarchs, spoiled brat billionaires, and "gentleman" mobsters with a taste for finer things. His testimony against them nearly got him killed and led to death threats that Ben and Erik took seriously, even now.

"Gotta love New Jersey." Erik sighed. "Come for the beaches, sleep with the fishes."

"I'll take the chips downstairs and put them in the safe," Susan volunteered. "We can look into the provenance later. I'm sorry to spoil your move-in."

Erik shook his head. "No harm done. Maybe Jaxon knows more about the casino?" Jaxon Davies ran the Cape May Center for the Arts, which devoted itself to the area's history. "It seems like Jaxon knows everything about anything local."

"It's worth asking. You haven't stopped in to see him in a while," Ben noted.

After Susan left, Ben and Erik sat down to eat. The casserole was as good as it smelled, and after a day of hauling boxes, they dug in realizing they were hungrier than they had thought.

Later, they curled up on the couch with wine to watch a movie. Ben leaned against Erik's shoulder. "Any other thoughts about today?"

Erik pressed his lips against Ben's temple. "Just how much I love knowing that you live here with me. I'm the psychometric, remember? So your possessions have your vibes. Your resonance is stronger now that your things are here. I like the shift in the apartment's energy. Plus, you're inside the wardings. I can protect you better."

"Don't bruise my city cop ego," Ben teased. "I know how to be armed and dangerous."

Erik's hand slipped down to cup Ben's crotch, and Ben felt his dick twitch in response. "Hmm. You're definitely packing heat."

"You know what I meant."

Erik kissed the top of his head. "I do. And I didn't mean any disrespect for your manhood, which I'm very fond of." He continued to stroke Ben's crotch as his cock filled. "But the magical wardings are stronger on the store and apartment than I was able to create on your old place since it was a rental. Magic is strange like that."

Before he moved to Cape May, Ben would have doubted the reality of spells, curses, and warding, even with a grandmother who was said to be able to put the Evil Eye on people she didn't like. Since moving to one of the most haunted towns in North America and dealing with vengeful ghosts and murderous witches, Ben had become a true believer in the supernatural.

Erik's store Trinkets had operated for well over a century, passing from one long-time owner to the next. While most antique shops occasionally encountered unlucky or haunted objects, Trinkets had a mission to get dangerous supernatural objects out of the wrong hands.

Like the previous proprietors, Erik had agreed to continue the store's purpose, coordinating with the Alliance, a coalition of mortals and immortals who helped keep the world safe from paranormal threats. Part of that heritage included exceptionally strong protections on the store and the house, extending to the apartment.

Ben had seen those protections in action.

"We could take this into the bedroom, and I'll let you get into my holster," Ben teased, sliding his hand under Erik's shirt and up his chest, lightly tweaking his nipples.

"I can't believe you said that," Erik groaned. "Did we suddenly end up in a cheesy porn?"

"I'll have you know that we would be a high-class example of adult entertainment," Ben said with mock indignation. "Cheesy porn indeed!"

"Shut up and kiss me," Erik murmured, angling Ben's face to press their lips together as his fingers worked the button and zipper of his pants.

"Bed. Now," Ben panted when they moved apart.

They shed clothing as they stumbled toward the bedroom, kissing and fondling as they went. Despite the apartment having several pieces of antique furniture, the bed was new and king-sized.

Erik backed Ben up to the foot of the bed, and they collapsed together onto the mattress. Ben flipped them with a triumphant grin, landing on top and straddling Erik's hips, grinding their erections together through damp briefs.

"God, you're beautiful." Ben enjoyed the view. He let his hands slide down Erik's sides, making the other man shiver, and wriggled backward, taking Erik's briefs with him.

Ben swallowed Erik down to the root, swirling his tongue and sucking. Erik caught his breath sharply, and his hips jerked. Ben pushed his lover's legs apart for better access and set up a rhythm as one hand stilled Erik's hips and the other slid underneath to stroke his balls.

"So good...you just know...oh, God," Erik panted.

Ben worked him sloppy and wet, the way he knew Erik liked it. He hollowed his cheeks and sucked, then ran his tongue up the veiny underside and pressed into just the right place beneath the plump head before sliding the tip through Erik's slit. When he slid two fingers back along Erik's taint and found his hole, still open from when they fucked earlier that morning, he slipped inside and pressed on that magic spot as he took Erik's cock into his throat.

Erik's fingers gripped Ben's hair as his body arched and his dick pulsed. Ben swallowed it all, working Erik through the aftershocks, and pulled off with a *pop*.

"Liked that?" he asked, voice roughened from deepthroating. He gave a kitten flick of his tongue against the head of Erik's cock and felt his lover tremble.

"Let me return the favor." Erik tugged Ben up until his knees were at Erik's shoulders, and Erik could pull him into his mouth.

Ben gripped the headboard as Erik dug his fingers into Ben's ass, urging him forward. Between the suction and the way Erik's tongue worshipped his cock, Ben knew he wouldn't last long.

He came hard, jizz spilling out of the corners of Erik's mouth, leaking down his chin and neck as the rhythm of Ben's hips stuttered, and he gasped with his release.

A playful slap on the ass pulled Ben out of his post-orgasm haze, and he sat back on his haunches. Erik looked utterly debauched, mouth sticky with Ben's come, hair mussed and wild, lips reddened and puffy from being used.

I did that. He looks like that because of me.

"I love you. That rocked. Now stop sitting on my chest so I can breathe." Erik rolled, tumbling Ben to the side.

Ben stretched up to lick the spunk from Erik's throat and then kissed him so that Erik could taste himself on Ben's tongue.

"Love you too," Ben managed in a fucked-out growl. He went to the bathroom to clean off and returned with a wet cloth to wipe Erik down, then tossed the washcloth toward the door and pulled the covers up over both of them.

"Thanks for making me feel at home." Ben rested his head on Erik's shoulder.

Erik wrapped his arms around Ben. "That's because you *are* home. We're home when we're together."

As he drifted off to sleep, Ben thought about the poker chips. He tightened his grip on Erik and sent a silent wish to anyone listening to keep his lover safe.

TWO

ERIK

Erik saw Ben off to work with a kiss and a slap on the ass after waking him up with a "good morning" hand job.

He lingered over a cup of coffee since his "commute" involved a single flight of stairs. Erik replayed the events of the night before, not just the pleasure but the look in Ben's eyes, the way it felt to be the focus of his intense attention, the sound of his voice.

I thought I was in love before, but that was nothing like this. When he left Atlanta, Erik thought his world had come to an end, disillusioned and heartbroken, only to discover the chance to make something much better here.

He thought about the chaos of moving Ben into the apartment and their odd mix of décor. A very small part of him chafed a little at the disruption. There were parts of living alone—like getting his way about everything since there was no one else to consider—that were easy. He forgot the effort that went into compromise. But he had meant what he'd told Ben—having them live together outweighed any minor adjustments.

Will we drive each other nuts? Have I gotten too set in my ways? Will all those endearing "quirks" we both have become annoying as hell now that we're together all the time?

Erik reached out and picked up a coaster that had been part of Ben's kitchen supplies. The resonance of Ben's energy immediately enfolded him, a calming and supportive vibe.

That's why I know he's "it" for me. It's never been like that with anyone else. So I'm going to pull on my big boy pants and do whatever I need to do to make this last.

He still had more than an hour before the shop opened, so he refilled his mug and powered up his laptop. Erik logged into his blog, appropriately named Treasure Trail, and glanced at the comments on his most recent post, then sat back and thought about what he wanted to write.

When he moved to Cape May, Erik had nixed the opportunity to do a television show with the local PBS station about antiques. He hadn't forgotten that his work with law enforcement had made him some powerful enemies who were bound to hold grudges. That hadn't forced him into WITSEC—although the idea had been seriously suggested more than once—but in order to stay alive and keep his freedom, Erik voluntarily chose to keep a relatively low profile.

The blog was a compromise. He drew on his experience authenticating and appraising artwork, gearing the site toward collectors and serious decorators who valued history and provenance. The most popular posts invited readers to ask questions or post photos for discussion, like an unofficial online *Antiques Roadshow*.

Erik only did appraisals by appointment, but he could usually help fill in the blanks about the various pieces posted in the comments, giving the owners a better sense of whether the item might be truly valuable or was only important for sentimental reasons. His blog also kept him in front of collectors and decorators who were potential year-round customers after the tourists went home.

The odd poker chips sparked inspiration, and Erik decided to write about collectible amusement park souvenirs. New Jersey had been home to some of the oldest and most famous parks in the country, and while many of those venues had closed over the years, the legends and memories lived on in the memorabilia.

Palisades Park might have been gone for fifty years, but it was immortalized in a song that still played on the radio. Action Park remained infamous for its extreme thrill rides and questionable safety record. Olympic Park had been gone for decades, but its carousel got a new lease on life at Disney World.

Erik felt his enthusiasm rise as he wrote about the common and uncommon souvenirs that were all that were left of many parks. Ashtrays, trivets, mugs, and T-shirts vied with pressed pennies, wooden nickels, postcards, and etched glassware. Some fans even bought ride cars, merry-go-round horses, signage, and decorations from defunct parks.

He explained how the memorabilia was appraised, cautioning readers that most items held little monetary value although could be important for family or local history. Then on a whim, he asked readers for their memories about several now-closed parks that had once been in the Cape May area, including Fun Factory.

"Even if it doesn't turn up anything useful, it'll be a good discussion," he muttered as he uploaded his post. Fall was the tail end of tourist season, and he figured the post would remind readers of sunny days from past summers.

His phone reminded him that it was time to open the shop. Erik turned his laptop off before heading to unlock the door. Susan arrived moments later.

"It's definitely getting chilly out there." She shouldered out of her jacket and headed for the break room. Erik got the register ready while Susan brewed a fresh pot of coffee, which filled the air with its aroma.

"Do we have any amusement park pieces?" Erik asked when she returned to the front of the shop.

She chuckled. "Been thinking about those poker chips, haven't you?"

"Prompted a blog post, so that's already valuable," he admitted. "And it gave me an excuse to ask if anyone had heard of Fun Factory, among other long-ago parks. Having the chips show up just seems too strange to be random."

"Maybe not for anyone else, but for you—yes," Susan agreed. "And

I think the idea of putting out a blog post is perfect. You ought to pop in on Jaxon and see what he knows."

"Ben and I were just talking about that. Let's see how the day goes, and I'll find a way to fit in a visit today or tomorrow."

With his focus on Ben moving in, Erik had forgotten that he was due a shipment from an estate auction in a nearby town. Susan watched the front of the store while Erik worked his way through the crates, making sure to wear gloves in case any of his new purchases held more mojo than he expected.

Most of the items were mundane—a mantle clock, bookends, a vase by a noted local potter, and other decorative pieces dating to the late 1800s or early 1900s. He sighed with relief as he neared the bottom of the crate, then frowned as he saw a small item wrapped in brown paper he didn't remember purchasing.

Holding his hand above the package made it clear there was resonance, although Erik didn't sense a threat. He reached for the silver tongs he used for just such an occasion, pulling at the wrapping until the paper tore to reveal the item inside.

"Shit."

The dessert plate bore the insignia of the Commodore Wilson Hotel.

"Something wrong?" Susan ventured into the break room, standing so she could still keep an eye on the outer door. For the moment, no customers milled about inside.

"Have a look." Erik stepped back, and Susan peered into the crate.

"Uh-oh." She managed a brave smile. "Maybe it's just a plate. Nothing special."

Erik shook his head. "No, I can feel the energy. I should bring Alessia Mason in on this. Maybe her coven has an update on the hotel."

"The hotel that's been gone for almost thirty years?" Susan raised an eyebrow.

"I think we proved the last time that the Commodore Wilson isn't an 'average' hotel. Or really gone."

The grand hotel was intended to attract wealthy families who usually summered in the Hamptons or Nantucket. At the time it was built in the early 1900s, it was the largest in the world, designed for luxury. A Tiffany ceiling dome, marble floors, and a sweeping staircase welcomed visitors to the ornate lobby. It boasted an indoor pool, a bowling alley, a grand ballroom, and more than three hundred guest rooms.

Yet the project seemed snakebit, an albatross that pushed every owner into ruin. Construction ran late and well over budget. The Stock Market Crash of 1929 depleted the fortunes of its owner and the high-end customers it sought. The Commodore Wilson changed hands again and again, often owned by dreamers and scoundrels, including some with ties to the Mob. More than one murder or tragic death left a stain on its energy as neglect wore away at the structure. The old hotel had been deemed too expensive to repair, and explosives turned it into rubble.

The problem was the Commodore Wilson Hotel never actually left.

The land remained empty since deal after deal fell through despite its prime oceanfront location. On nights when the veil between the normal world and the supernatural thinned, those with abilities saw the "ghost" of the old hotel, like an image burned into the space it used to inhabit.

The whole thing gave Erik the creeps, especially since he and Ben had already dealt with unhappy ghosts, unfinished Mob business, and unsettled grudges from the glory days of the infamous hotel.

Erik wasn't thrilled about a rematch, but it looked like one was coming.

"Okay," he said. "Let me work through the 'special' pieces in the back, and then I'll give Alessia a call and see what she knows about this whole mess."

"What about the man who used to own Trinkets, the one you bought the store from?" Susan asked. "He was older and might know about the Fun Factory, even if it was before he lived here; it would be closer to his time."

"You're brilliant," Erik said with a grin. "That's a great idea."

Susan went up front when the bell above the door jingled, and Erik headed to the back room, closing the door behind him. He poured another cup of coffee and closed his eyes, taking a few deep breaths to settle his nerves and center his psychic ability. Then he pulled on cotton gloves that had silver threads running through them to help blunt supernatural mojo and set a locked wooden box on the break room table.

The box had runes and sigils from a variety of magical traditions carved into its wood and silver. Erik worked the lock and opened the lid, no longer remembering what pieces he had set aside for later inspection.

Anything that triggered his touch magic went into the box until he could verify whether it was dangerous and if so, whether it could be cleansed or needed special disposal.

Erik grabbed a canister of salt and put down a line across the doorway so nothing could leave the room, then he made a circle around the table and chair, a protective barrier that would keep ghosts and some magic from leaving the warded area. He set down another, smaller circle around his chair for his own protection, in addition to the silver, agate, and onyx charms he wore as a matter of course. He didn't think the items in the box were particularly dangerous, but he had been wrong before, so he didn't take chances.

The first item Erik withdrew was a gold locket on a chain. The initials "C R" were etched on the front in a filigree font. Erik closed his eyes and let his senses read the piece. He picked up sadness and longing but nothing malicious. A note he'd placed with the locket reminded him that it had been sold to the shop by the granddaughter of the owner, a woman named Catherine, who had recently passed away in her nineties.

Erik opened the locket to reveal two black and white photographs of a young man and woman. From their hairstyles and clothing, he guessed the period to be the early 1950s.

"I know you're there, Catherine," he murmured to the ghost he sensed just out of sight. "Why have you stayed behind?"

The air grew cold enough for Erik to see his breath. His skin prickled, and the hair on the back of his neck stood up, warning him that the spirit had drawn closer. She wasn't strong enough to make herself seen, but Erik glimpsed her image in his mind. Catherine appeared as she must have looked when she died, old and fragile, not the young woman in the locket.

"Stay behind? Where should I go? I just went to sleep, and when I woke up, everyone was gone. Do you know the way?"

Erik felt a pang of compassion for the woman's spirit. Despite the energy that clung to the locket from her revenant, she posed no threat.

In his experience, and from what he understood from people who were actual mediums, most spirits went on to the afterlife unassisted. A few resisted leaving the mortal world, usually because of unfinished business or the need to protect loved ones. Some clung to this world out of fear of what the next might hold.

Others, like Catherine, just took a "wrong turn."

"Would you like me to show you the way?" He gave an encouraging smile.

"Yes, please. I'm very tired."

Erik closed his eyes and concentrated on her faint energy as he spoke words of blessing, giving encouragement and permission to move on.

In his mind's eye, Erik saw the ghost take on a faint glow. Her expression turned from discomfort to astonishment.

"Oh. That's it. Thank you so much." Catherine turned and faded into the glow that had limned her form.

"Go in peace, Catherine," Erik murmured. He reached for the cup of coffee he had set nearby, needing the caffeine and sugar to replenish his energy.

The next piece was a palm-sized, cream colored porcelain swan edged in gold. Erik guessed it might have held mints or a personal serving of sugar in its open back. He didn't sense any harm or actual ghosts, just deep wistfulness and the faint image of a long-ago wedding.

Most people didn't realize how much the objects around them

soaked up their emotions. When they found an item at a flea market or curio shop that seemed to pull them in, they were reacting on a subconscious level to that emotional resonance. And when someone shied away from an heirloom because it "gave them the creeps," the same was true.

Erik had long believed that the majority of people had some level of psychic sensitivity, something that usually got brushed off as intuition or imagination. They were either attracted or repelled by pre-owned items without ever knowing why. Those who picked up no resonance at all were the ones who could own objects with checkered pasts and never seemed to notice.

For the swan dish, Erik tried a simple cleansing litany, saying the words as he lit a candle and burned protective herbs in a chalice. He let the smoke from the herbs gather around the swan and passed the candle flame back and forth over the piece. The emotions gradually drained away, leaving the figurine inert—harmless and ethical to resell.

Erik reached into the box and found the next item—a man's ring. The large square garnet looked blood red against its gold setting. Erik picked up the piece and shuddered despite his protective gloves.

While the ring was well-crafted and the stone valuable, Erik knew immediately why it had ended up in the box. The emotions oozing from the jewelry were thick with anger, jealousy, and vindictiveness. Whoever had worn the ring had been desperately unhappy, filled with rage, and convinced they had been cheated by life.

Erik caught his breath at the strength of the emotions and recoiled when he realized that it also came with a faded ghost.

The florid-faced man looked to be in his late seventies, with a fringe of gray hair and bushy eyebrows. He had broad shoulders and a barrel chest, and from his stance, Erik figured the man was used to shoving and pushing his way through life.

"Who are you?" the ghost demanded, noticing Erik. *"Fix this immediately. I can't be dead. I have a board meeting."*

Whatever appointment the spirit wanted to keep was likely fifty years long gone.

"You're dead," Erik told him. "I can help you move on, but I can't send you back."

"If you can't fix this, get me someone who can. I'm a very busy man."

"You can remain tied to your ring or move on to the afterlife. Those are your only choices."

The spirit let out a howl of rage and flung itself toward Erik. Erik recoiled although his salt barrier stopped the angry ghost before it could reach him.

The specter hurled himself against the warding, cursing and shrieking. Erik drew a calming breath and began to recite a banishment ritual, adding more leaves to those in the chalice and wafting the smoke toward the ghost.

"You no longer have a claim to this world. It is time to leave this realm and move on. Be gone, angry soul, and trouble this place no more."

If the man hadn't already been dead, apoplexy probably would have killed him. He grew red in the face, spewing threats and raising his fist against the barrier.

Erik saw when the banishment took hold, thinning the ghost's outline and muffling his shouts. Seconds later, the spirit seemed to realize it too, and his eyes widened in fear.

"What's going on? You can't do this! I deserve more time. I demand you change—"

The ghost vanished between one blink and the next in silence, not even a faint *pop* to mark his passing.

"Go in peace and trouble the living no more." Erik gulped his coffee and reached for the candy bar he kept handy for this type of work. After he had finished both, he felt fortified enough to face the last two pieces.

The first was the Commodore Wilson plate from that day's shipment. Erik examined the dish carefully and frowned. He had seen many other serving pieces from the old hotel since auctioning off its inventory had been a major event in Cape May.

This plate looked slightly different. It still had the blue band around the outer edge and the elaborate "CW" monogram in the center. But this had traces of gold outlining both the design in the middle and the rim. Erik wondered if it had been reserved for VIP guests or the executive management.

When he held the plate, Erik felt a tangle of emotions: pride, uneasiness, irritation, and a deep sense of foreboding flooded his senses. He caught fragmentary glimpses of meals and meetings, of dour men in suits, and heated arguments. Few of the people were in focus enough to identify, but the face of the person most connected to the plate burned into Erik's memory.

I've seen him before. He was one of the early owners of the hotel.

He saw the faintly familiar person arguing with another man who looked like a 1920s' mobster straight out of Hollywood central casting.

Interesting connection. What does it mean, and why was it strong enough to persist?

He waited for a moment to see if a ghost would show up. When none did, Erik considered his options. He could cleanse the piece, and that would probably wipe its resonance free.

If we're going to get dragged into something involving the Commodore Wilson, we might need to see if there's more information we could glean from this. I can always cleanse it later.

Erik wrapped the plate in a spelled cloth to dampen its energy and put it back in the warded box. *Maybe with the equinox coming, the resonance got a power boost. It's not dangerous, but I wonder if it's important.*

That left the Fun Factory poker chips.

This time, Erik didn't shy away from the impressions he received. In the background, a sense of excitement and a glimpse of bright lights along with strains of calliope music. As he held the chips, he picked up tension and wondered if the markers had been part of a high-stakes game.

A shot rang out, making Erik jump before he realized it was a long-ago memory. He saw flashes of frantic movement, smelled fresh blood, and heard a woman scream.

He dropped the chips and tried to calm his thudding heart. The resonance left no question in his mind that something had gone very wrong, like a robbery or a murder at a casino.

When Erik had first seen the chips, he imagined an early version of Coney Island from the name. But something had teased at the back of his mind because he couldn't quite square poker with carousels. The image he just saw made him doubt that guess, since the impression looked more like something from a casino than an amusement park.

He opted not to cleanse the chips, thinking they might find more clues once he knew what to look for.

Erik wrapped the chips and put them into the box, which he placed in the heavy iron safe, heavily warded and covered with runes. Pieces that were beyond Erik's ability to neutralize or that were actively malicious were set aside for Sorren, his contact with the Alliance, to pick up and deal with.

Erik dispelled the wardings and swept up the salt, put out the candles, and blessed the ashes of the burned herbs. Then he drank a Coke and took a few minutes to collect himself before he reached for his phone.

"Mr. Pettis?" he said when he heard a voice on the other end. "It's Erik Mitchell."

"Erik—good to hear from you. And please, call me Robert."

"How's Charleston?" Erik asked. After Pettis sold Trinkets, he moved to Charleston, South Carolina, with his nephew Chuck.

Before owning the shop, Robert Pettis had worked for a secretive and questionable government organization that fought supernatural dangers. The organization, C.H.A.R.O.N., took an aggressive approach that tended to leave collateral damage in its wake and lingering doubts about its methods.

Chuck had also worked for C.H.A.R.O.N., though he and his uncle left disillusioned and regretful. Sorren had used his influence to give them sanctuary in Charleston, a city that the nearly six-hundred-year-old vampire considered to be under his protection.

All of which meant that Robert was even better versed in the occult and its remedies than Erik.

"You lived in Cape May for a long time. Did you ever hear of a place called the Fun Factory?"

"Huh," Robert grunted. "Let me think. I seem to recall the name, but whatever it was had been gone before I got there. Some sort of entertainment complex maybe, around the turn of the last century. It wasn't in Cape May proper. I'm thinking Sewell's Point, although I could be wrong."

He cleared his throat. "Don't know if that was any help, but if I think of something else, I can let you know. How did that come up?"

Erik told him about the mysterious poker chips and the reading he had gotten from them.

"Interesting," Robert mused. "Reminds me of why I retired. I'm too old for that sort of shit."

Erik chuckled. "Some days, I think I am too."

"Was that all you needed?" Robert had a gruff way of speaking, but Erik had learned not to take it personally.

"I think so," Erik replied. "Thanks for your time."

"Like I said, if I remember anything about that place, I'll let you know," Robert replied. "Watch your back. This stuff is never simple."

Erik ended the call and sat for a moment staring at his darkened phone. He finished his now-cold coffee, lost in thought about the objects he had handled from the box.

He might not be able to find out who sent the poker chips, but clearly a story lay behind them and some sort of tragedy. Loose ends and unfinished business often ended up biting him in the ass—in an extremely unsexy way.

"Everything go okay?" Susan asked when Erik emerged from the back room. One customer milled around the shop, typical now that it was the off-season.

"I'm going to drop in on Alessia." Erik grabbed his jacket. "If she's too busy to talk, at least I can stretch my legs and clear my head."

"Have fun," Susan replied. "And I want to hear all about what you saw from the stuff in the box when you get back."

Alessia Mason owned the Spirit of the Sea gift shop, not far from

Trinkets. A brisk wind came off the ocean, and Erik turned up his collar against the chill.

This was his first fall in Cape May. Atlanta didn't really have "tourist season" in the same way as a beachfront resort town. In Atlanta, a steady calendar of conventions, sporting events, concerts, and more meant visitors year-round, without an off time. By comparison, Cape May seemed quiet, even a bit sleepy, when the vacationers headed home. Some shops and restaurants cut back on hours or closed for part of the winter while the owners presumably headed for warmer climes.

Erik hoped that his blog and the relationships he cultivated with decorators and collectors would keep the shop in the black during the winter. Business had grown throughout the summer and so far remained steady. He crossed his fingers that a little ingenuity and marketing know-how would help him ride out the quieter months.

He felt a faint frisson of magic when he walked into the gift shop, not surprising since Alessia was a powerful witch. The store offered ocean-themed artwork and jewelry along with crystals, meditation aids, and books on Wicca and other paranormal subjects.

Alessia was finishing up a sale with a customer. Erik hung back, not wanting to interrupt, and browsed the shop's ever-changing selection of upscale gifts. He was already thinking ahead to Christmas and coming up with a list of ideas for Ben.

The door closed, and Alessia looked up from the register. "Hello, Erik. I've been expecting you."

Alessia Mason's olive skin and black hair played up her dark brown eyes, part of her Sicilian heritage. Like Erik, she was a transplant to Cape May, where she had married into one of the town's old, influential, and wealthy families. That might have afforded her an entrance to the Cape May business community and social scene, but she built the local coven all by herself.

She flipped the sign on the door to "Closed" and led Erik to the back room, where she made them cups of her special tea blend. Just the smell as it steeped eased Erik's tight shoulders and soothed the tension he hadn't realized he carried.

"I had a dream about you and a card game gone wrong." Alessia brought two steaming mugs to the table and settled into her chair. "So, spill. What's going on?"

Erik sighed and took in a deep breath of the fragrant tea. "I'm hoping you can tell me." He recapped what he knew about the poker chips and the mysterious Fun Factory.

"I tried the search engines," Erik confessed. "There wasn't much. I found a couple of mentions but few details. Robert Pettis thought it was in Sewell's Point but didn't know anything else off-hand."

"If you want to know about the Fun Factory, Jaxon's your best bet. My interest is the resonance of the chips. Violence, maybe a shooting, possibly a murder. Seems extreme for an amusement park."

"I've heard about some of the old-fashioned rides they had at those early parks," Erik replied, pausing to take a sip. "No safety inspections, so they were pretty wild. But what I saw seemed more like a casino than a midway."

"I'm wondering about the timing on the chips showing up now," Alessia said. "They've obviously been around for a long while."

Erik shrugged. "Someone might have been cleaning out an older relative's house or found them tucked in the bottom of a drawer. It happens."

Alessia gave him a look. "For those with supernatural gifts, very little occurs by chance. Especially since we're coming up on the Equinox. It's one of the dates with a strong pull on the genius loci."

"You mean the 'ghost' of the Commodore Wilson?"

She nodded. "Yes, although 'ghost' isn't quite the right term. Maybe 'essence' or 'resonance.' Or given its energy, perhaps 'stain' is closer," she added with a curl to her lip.

"If there's a link somehow between the poker chips and the Commodore Wilson, maybe that's why they've turned up now," Erik theorized. "There was also a gold-rimmed small plate with the hotel's monogram."

"Hmm. The plate would have been for the VIP dining room. I agree that there could be a link with the chips and the hotel. Although as you noted, the chips are old, and whatever happened occurred long ago. Interesting that it's waited until now to manifest."

Erik fought the urge to squirm in his chair. "I'd argue for coincidence, but I know you don't believe in that either."

"Clearly not. But I do believe in synchronicity, alignment, syzygy," Alessia replied.

"Isn't that last one when planets line up?" Erik knew he had heard the strange term somewhere.

She nodded. "Exactly. Maybe someone brought the chips back to Cape May, or they were dormant throughout the cycles that the old hotel's genius loci waxed and waned. All that's different this year, is you."

"That isn't exactly comforting," Erik muttered. "I'm not a witch. I can read energies and see ghosts, but I'm not even a full medium. Why me?"

She shrugged. "Sometimes what matters is finding someone who will listen."

Erik didn't think that was reassuring, although it made sense. How long had the poker chips gone unnoticed by people who were blind to their energy? While they weren't exactly haunted, Erik had the sense that there was a story urgently wanting to be told, enough so to cross decades.

"This kind of thing always opens a big can of worms," he said, condensing his train of thought.

Alessia gave a hearty laugh. "Oh, my dear Erik. That's the truth about all occult talents in a nutshell. Now, how are you going to deal with the worms?"

Erik grimaced. "I'm not sure yet. And I hope that this time, it doesn't involve either Ben or me getting shot. We've had entirely too much of that." He paused to drink the rest of his cooling tea. "Tell me more about the thing with the Commodore Wilson."

"The 'thing' is a genius loci—the spirit of a place—that either was always malicious or has gotten twisted. Maybe a little of both," Alessia recapped. Erik knew this much from prior conversations, but it always made his head hurt a little to try to fathom the idea.

"While it existed, the hotel seduced and then destroyed its builder and everyone who owned it," she continued. "That's why I think it has always had bad energy. Many of the people who heard its siren song weren't upstanding citizens—mobsters, fire-breathing evangelists, businessmen of dubious ethics. If the hotel's energy acted on them, then it's also possible that their...failings...echoed with that energy, which is where the 'twisted' part comes in."

"I thought the autumn equinox was about cleansing," Erik protested. "Why would the hotel's energy surge then?"

Alessia set aside her empty cup. "Every ritual has a dark side as well as a light side. We tend to speak more of the positives, but many old autumn traditions recognize the darkness of the human soul in contrast to the light. It's a commonality that stretches across time, location, and tradition. When something shows up in that many places to that many people, it's wise to pay attention."

"What can we do? You've already said that the energy can't be banished or cleansed." The longer they talked, the more Erik's stomach tightened with a sense of foreboding.

"It can't be eliminated—but it can be contained," Alessia stressed. "That's one of the primary responsibilities of the coven. We are the guardians who use all the assets at our disposal to minimize the damage the genius loci can inflict."

Sometimes people swore they saw the ghost of the Commodore Wilson on the barren lot where it once stood. Stories varied, with some claiming only to have seen the hotel's distinctive silhouette, while others said the building appeared nearly solid, although the illusion lasted only seconds.

The snake-bit history of the grand hotel was at odds with the fond memories of long-time Cape May residents who told of weddings, parties, engagements, and proms at the once-opulent venue. Despite its long decline into disrepair, locals spoke of the Commodore Wilson wistfully, with a wish it could have been saved despite the monumental expense of reversing the ravages of age and poor construction.

Its ghostly appearance had entered local folklore like a hometown version of Mercury in retrograde. Erik had heard people say things like, "it's been that kind of day—must be time for the Commodore to show up."

Having a massive, haunted—possibly cursed—spectral hotel appear and disappear on a regular basis would have seemed strange, but Erik reminded himself that Cape May was already one of the most haunted towns on the East Coast. People here just went with the flow.

"I don't think the poker chips are cursed," Erik said. "But there's definitely something…unresolved. And in my experience, loose ends are dangerous."

Alessia nodded. "True. So we need to take care of that. I'll see what I can find from my sources. Keep digging at yours. If the chips have surfaced now, they want resolution. That will attract the attention it seeks."

"What worries me is what else might get dragged along," Erik admitted. "It's never as simple as it looks."

Erik headed back to Trinkets with a couple of fresh protective hex bags for him and Ben and a promise that Alessia would put the word out to her contacts.

He closed his hand around the hex bags and felt a warm, calming presence. It soothed him, although he knew that charms, however powerful, wouldn't be sufficient to deflect the energy swell of the genius loci. He managed to push the troubling thoughts from his mind. Erik couldn't do anything about the Commodore Wilson, but the poker chips had started to feel like a personal quest.

I might not be able to tackle the biggest issue, but if I can defuse the smaller one, at least the two problems can't gang up on us.

The rest of the afternoon went quietly. Erik filled Susan in on what he had learned, and she assured him that she had spread the word about the Fun Factory to her network of contacts, which he sometimes thought included everyone in Cape May.

"I put in a call to Etta at the library and Steve at the archive," Susan told him. "They take it as a point of personal pride to know every-thing about the area's history. They might not learn anything about the owner of the chips, but you could find a clue in whatever they do turn up."

"Great idea—thank you," Erik said. "If we could narrow down the time period, there should be a police report of a shooting even if it didn't end up being a murder."

Susan nodded. "I thought about that. One step at a time." She glanced at her watch. "Didn't you say you were supposed to meet Ben for dinner? Go on ahead. I'll finish here."

Erik was surprised that the day had gone by so fast. He helped close the store and walked Susan to her house next door.

"Thanks for handling business so I could go off sleuthing," Erik said. "I couldn't do it without you."

"I can watch the register anytime so you can help save the world," she teased. "Now go meet up with that hunky boyfriend of yours, and don't waste your time talking shop."

Erik did his best to clear the day's worries from his mind as he walked several blocks to meet Ben at The Spike, a popular restaurant and bar that stayed open year-round.

The Spike was known as much for its live music, firepits, and perpetual cornhole challenges as it was for its menu. It was a local favorite for all those reasons, but it held a special place in Erik's heart for being where he and Ben met for the first time.

The memory made him smile even as Erik hunched against the cold. He'd been new in town, feeling lonely after leaving his old job and a bitter breakup with an unfaithful partner, and finally gave in and used a dating app. When he showed up at The Spike in the agreed-upon meeting place, Ben had taken the seat next to him, and they had struck up a conversation. They had immediate chemistry, giving Erik the mistaken impression that Ben was his date.

Unfortunately, that wasn't the case. The guy from the dating app was a complete bust, and when Erik saw Ben joking with another man, he concluded that Ben was already taken. It took a ghostly mobster and a haunted clock to finally get them together.

The glow of the firepits cheered Erik as The Spike came into view.

He stepped into the lobby to warm up at the large hearth before venturing to the outdoor bar.

"Come here often?" he said in his most seductive voice as he sidled up to Ben, taking the barstool next to him.

"Only with my sexy boyfriend." Ben reached over to give Erik's knee a squeeze. "Good thing you got here on time—I'm cold enough to be a popsicle."

That put all kinds of naughty images in Erik's mind, and Ben's smirk confirmed that to be his intention.

"I like popsicles." Erik held Ben's gaze. "I was counting on licking one tonight."

"None of that canoodling," Sherry Weller, The Spike's owner teased. "This is a respectable bar."

"Since when?" Ben joked.

"Well, before you two walked in," she shot back. Sherry and her wife Jo took a hands-on approach to running the venue and were usually behind the bar if they didn't have to pinch-hit elsewhere.

"I'll take an Irish coffee," Erik ordered. "It's cold out here."

"Make that two." Ben turned back to Erik. "I put in a request for an indoor table, and we can stand next to the firepits while we wait."

They took their drinks to the circle of light and warmth from the large iron firepits circled by Adirondack chairs. Off to one side, the cornhole games were lively despite the chill. Erik noted that the night's musician had set up at the inside bar, probably to avoid being too cold to sing.

He tightened his grip on the mug with one hand and reached over to take Ben's hand with the other. "How was today?"

Ben shrugged. "Things went okay. Since it's the off-season, that means repairs, remodeling, and touch-ups. We've already made a list of which units need work. Now I get to prioritize what starts first. There are a lot of properties. It's going to take until next summer to work through them all."

Erik smiled. It wasn't hard to picture Ben as a Newark cop or as a private investigator. He had the body for a uniform and the looks to be a noir sleuth. His current job required polo shirts with the rental company logo and khaki pants, which always made Erik think Ben was undercover.

"You'll do a great job. After all, you've been doing a lot of the hands-on stuff since you were a teenager, right?" Erik replied.

"Yeah. Sean and I worked summers for my aunt and uncle. We did the do-it-yourself stuff that didn't require special training—pulling up carpet, painting, swapping out light fixtures."

"I always had a handyman fantasy." Erik leaned close to Ben's ear. "Have I mentioned you look good in a tool belt?"

Ben gave his hand a playful squeeze. "I'm happy to nail you anytime," he said in a low voice.

"And we're back to cheesy porn." Erik laughed.

"Seriously—it was great experience doing all those odd jobs," Ben said. "Unclogging toilets and stopped-up sinks, stripping and hanging wallpaper, painting rooms, sanding, and re-staining cabinets. A million other things like that. Saved my aunt and uncle a bundle and definitely gave Sean and me usable life skills."

"Which explains why Sean now runs a food truck?"

Ben sighed. "Sean wanted to get out of Cape May. I know that Wildwood isn't actually that far away, but it's a completely different vibe."

"Oh, I could see that when we visited," Erik agreed. "I think the difference is that you and I had all the excitement we could handle before we came to Cape May. Sean's still looking for his."

Ben rolled his eyes. "I'm all for less excitement." Both he and Erik had gunshot scars as souvenirs of their past.

Cape May, with its Victorian homes and upscale shops, still had a Gilded Age sense about it. Wildwood, by comparison, was amusement parks, beach fun, and food festivals, drawing a younger and much less sedate crowd. Atlantic City, farther up the coast, was famed for its casinos but had gotten rough around the edges of late.

"Actually, Sean called yesterday," Ben said. "He's coming down—sans food truck—to see friends, and we're going to lunch tomorrow."

"Tell him 'hi' for me," Erik said. "I hope business is still good for him?"

"So good he's weighing whether to get a second truck," Ben replied. Sean's specialty onion ring truck, *Put A Ring On It*, had found a sweet spot with Wildwood boardwalk visitors.

"Do you think he'll do it?" Erik hadn't pictured Ben's laid-back cousin as an empire-builder.

"Dunno. Sean works his ass off with the one truck, even with a crew. He always said he wanted enough money to be able to do the things he enjoyed and not worry but also not be too tied down. Which is why I'm the one running his parents' rental business now, with his blessing," Ben answered.

"You're welcome to join us," Ben added.

Erik shook his head. "I'm having lunch with Jaxon, and after that, I'm heading to the library and the archive."

"Chasing down those poker chips?"

Erik nodded. "I can't shake the feeling they're important. And if something wicked is coming this way—again—I want to be prepared."

Ben's beeper went off, and they headed inside. It seemed like a perfect night for the restaurant's signature burger, loaded with three different kinds of cheese and crispy fried onions. Erik ordered an appetizer plate of fried pickles, mac and cheese bites, and clam strips.

Over dinner, both men made an effort not to talk about work. Erik knew that Ben felt stressed about proving to his aunt and uncle that he could run the business well, even though their belief in him lay behind the offer to take over the company.

Plus a new relationship and moving in...and then the craziness of the past few months. That's a lot to juggle.

Erik was in the same boat, learning to run a business despite his background in antiquities. Not to mention having hit men, government agents, and rival Mafiosi after them. When he thought of it that way, Erik wondered how they'd managed as well as they had.

They ordered hot chocolate with Kahlua and Bailey's for dessert. Warmed by the drinks and full of good food, Ben and Erik enjoyed the starlit walk home despite the bracing ocean wind.

"When you go to the library, ask for Etta Campbell," Ben said. "She's been the reference librarian since I was a teenager, and she knows *everything*. Tell her I sent you. She helped me research how to get into the police academy back in the day."

Erik filled Ben in on the rest of his day—the troublesome objects and angry ghosts, the impressions he got from the poker chips and the plate, and his meeting with Alessia.

"So it's back?"

Erik knew Ben meant the Commodore Wilson. "Yeah, or rather, it's coming. That's why I hope that digging into the history of those pieces might give us an advantage when the shit hits the fan."

Ben turned to look Erik in the eye. "Don't take any crazy chances. I mean it. It's not our job to save the world."

"If not us, then who?" Erik replied, and Ben looked away. "Look, I'm not trying to be a hero. I didn't go looking for trouble. But this kinda landed in my lap, so trying to pretend we're not involved isn't going to work. And we're not alone. We've got friends. As long as we all stick together, we'll be okay."

He saw the skepticism in Ben's eyes and knew his boyfriend worried. Given the events of the recent past, Ben's concern wasn't paranoid. As much as he sometimes accused Ben of mother henning, his concern warmed Erik's heart, especially considering the lack of interest in his welfare shown by his prior boyfriend.

"We're just getting started," he told Ben, reeling him closer and face to face. The few inches difference in their height made Erik need to look up, something that always revved his motor. "I have lots of plans for us. Not going to risk that."

In Ben's gaze he saw love, worry, and a dash of fear that made him want to kiss his boyfriend until nothing remained except bliss.

"Come on. Let's get home." Erik tugged on Ben's hand. "I've got ideas on how to warm you up."

Erik knew the conversation wasn't over. He hoped his desire to avoid trouble didn't turn out to be wishful thinking.

THREE

BEN

"And that's how we ended up in a viral video." Sean Meirlach, Ben's cousin, finished his wildly unlikely story with a hearty laugh. "And here's the proof." He pulled out his phone and showed Ben a clip involving mistaken identity, two B-list celebrities, and his onion ring truck.

"That's a great shot of the truck. You can read the whole name. Was it good for business?" Ben asked when he stopped laughing.

"Sure was. And I swear to God I had nothing to do with making it happen. Kinda like that news segment last year. You couldn't come up with that sort of thing in a million years, but sometimes it works out."

Sean had mounted a crazy impromptu rescue by blaring the sound system of his food truck, turning on its disco ball lighting, and careening into the middle of two warring Mob families to save Ben. The truck had gained a few bullet holes, which Sean said gave it "street cred," especially when a local reporter put the whole wild story on the evening news.

"You still loving the life?" Ben asked. They were hanging out in the kitchen of the real estate office, a place that felt like home to both of them. Wrappers for their takeout subs littered the table.

"Absolutely. I know you've found what you needed here in Cape

May, and I'm happy for you, dude, but I just never fit here." Sean looked away as he took a sip of his Coke.

"Nothing wrong with going where you should be." Ben raised a mock toast with his soda. "I never figured all those summers ago that I'd leave the 'big city' and settle here, but...I guess if you're lucky, you find what you need."

"Didn't the Rolling Stones sing about that?"

"Shut up." Ben's fondness took the sting from his words. "Find anyone you wanted to keep for more than one night?"

"Not ready to slow my roll yet," Sean replied.

"God, you are so Jersey."

Sean loved to play the field, and since he was pansexual that field was broad.

"I'm having a good time." Sean dropped the macho front. "Darius, Matteo, and Taylor are awesome bros to room with. It's not perfect, but it's the wild teenage years I didn't get to have when I *was* a teenager."

Ben had escaped problems at home with an overly religious and homophobic mother and an equally unaccepting stepdad by spending as much time as possible with his Aunt Meg and Uncle Stewart in Cape May. He'd gone into the police academy as soon as he was old enough and felt like he had lived several lives in the years after that on the tough streets of Newark.

At the time, he'd envied Sean his protected life, and felt tremendously grateful that Meg and Stewart took him in for long stretches at a time. But he'd always known that Sean chafed at the same protections Ben had craved.

"Just don't piss off any more mobsters," Ben cautioned.

Sean laughed. "Look who's talking." He drained his Coke. "So...you and Erik. How's it going?" He exaggerated taking a look at Ben's hands. "I see he hasn't 'put a ring on it' yet."

Ben couldn't help the warm smile that came in response. "Not yet. Give it time."

Sean leaned forward. "Do tell."

Ben smacked Sean's arm with a half-hearted backhand. "No juicy details for you if that's what you're angling for."

"You two could rake in a second income online. Neither of you break mirrors," Sean volunteered.

"Eww. I'm going to pretend you didn't say that," Ben bantered. *Just what we need—wiseguys from our past seeing us doing the deed on the internet.*

"Everyone has a side hustle."

"I don't want to know," Ben replied, and he really didn't, although he could totally believe Sean flirted with online fame.

"I wasn't going to tell you. You'd tell my mom."

"You're a grown-ass adult," Ben returned. "Not her business. Not mine, either. But now I need to bleach my brain."

"Back to you and Erik—"

"So far, so good," Ben said. "I moved the rest of my stuff into the apartment. That makes it seem less like I'm just sleeping over, and I love spending more time together. It's just strange. Caleb and I had been together longer, but we never moved in together. It never seemed to be the right time. But with Erik, it didn't feel like we were rushing it."

"Keep your monogamous cooties to yourself." Sean pretended to brush bugs off his arm. "But seriously—I'm happy for both of you. You deserve someone like Erik. He makes you happy?"

Ben nodded. "He does. I'm still rather gobsmacked that he loves me back. I'm punching above my weight class."

Sean gave him a look. "Are you serious? First off, much as it pains me to say it, the two of you are equally attractive. Even if, when you were a kid, you looked like that possum that lived behind the dumpster."

"Hey—"

"It was the ears. You grew into them," Sean assured him.

"Thanks for that. I'll need therapy."

"You already needed therapy."

"I'll need more." Ben sighed. "I'm trying not to overthink this thing with Erik. We get along great. When something goes wrong, we talk it out. Neither one of us do toxic shit. I know he's not going to cheat on me, and I'd never betray his trust. We're comfortable just watching television or reading without 'doing' anything. It's perfect. Which freaks me out a little."

Sean's eyebrow quirked up. "You're freaked because it's too good?"

"I know it's crazy, but I spent years not believing I could ever have things work out right," Ben confessed. Sean was his oldest and closest confidante, and while their lives had taken different directions, Erik was the only person he trusted as much as his cousin.

"I mean, Erik used to travel the world. He worked for major museums and got called in on high-profile cases. I'm just a guy from Newark."

"Except Erik wasn't doing publicity tours. He was busting big-time bad guys with really powerful connections," Sean pointed out. "So you both had the same job—nailing sleazebags. His just had more Benjamins to throw around."

"I didn't say the feelings were rational," Ben replied. "Just owning my shit. Like telling myself that it was okay to take up space in the apartment. I kept trying to squeeze into small corners so I didn't overwhelm."

"That's Caleb in your head," Sean pointed out. "He was always getting on you about your comics stuff being 'silly' and 'too expensive' and 'taking up too much room.' Bounce that bastard right out of your brain. If you're going to live with Erik, then the apartment has to be home for both of you."

"I know—and that's what Erik's gone out of his way to point out. Bad habits are hard to unlearn."

Sean leaned in. "Dude. You two haven't been together a whole year yet, and you've both risked your lives to save each other from the fuckin' *Mafia*. I haven't met anyone I'd risk a parking ticket for. Why are you worried about where to hang your Comic-Con art? He's over the moon for you, and you're so damn smitten it's sorta disgusting. Quit worrying and just enjoy it. You've earned some good karma."

"I guess so." Ben believed what Sean told him, but he had to argue with his own insecurity and inner critic to accept that something good had finally come his way.

"Here's the part that matters—you're both good guys." Sean leaned back in his chair. "You're real. I see plenty of posers on the boardwalk and in the clubs. You two know who you are, and you're okay with it —and with each other. Not trying to pretend to be something you aren't, or change the other person. That's rare. You're lucky. So don't be a dumbass and screw it up."

Ben understood the affection beneath the snark. "Yeah, yeah. That's probably your whole year's worth of caring and sharing. But… thanks." He paused. "So…how are Aunt Meg and Uncle Stewart?"

Sean looked relieved at the change of topic. He crumpled his can of Coke after draining the very last drops and set it on the table, idly spinning it back and forth with his finger.

"They're real good. Took a cruise to Alaska and then went down to Bermuda. I think they want to go on that train that crosses Canada, and the last time I was home, Mom had brochures from some paddle-wheeler that goes down the Mississippi. Living their best lives."

"Good for them," Ben said. "I hope they know I want to see pictures."

"I will pass that along."

Ben had been putting off the question he wanted to ask and couldn't delay any longer. "You hear any rumors about the Mob lately?"

Sean gave him a look. "I thought you were going to quit being a cop."

"I am. I have. It's just that stuff keeps finding us," Ben admitted. He told Sean about the poker chips, leaving out the woo-woo aspects about the mysterious hotel and malevolent genius loci for now.

"You just can't help stepping in it, can you?" Sean shook his head. "Actually, it's been fairly quiet on that angle. The guys who threatened to rough up my truck got caught, and after you and Erik pulled that big crazy showdown, the mobsters shaking down the food vendors are either too intimidated or too embarrassed to show their faces."

"Nothing about old casinos?"

"Nope. Unless you mean the ones in Atlantic City that keep trying to stay relevant. Given the age of their customers, they'd probably do well adding an assisted living wing."

"Can't take you out in public with a mouth like that." Ben sighed, although he appreciated Sean's inappropriate humor.

Sean started to say something, probably about other uses for his mouth, and Ben held up a hand.

"Don't say it. Just…don't."

"Made you think it though, didn't I?" Sean's eyes gleamed with nefarious glee.

"You're incorrigible."

"I'd agree, but I don't think I can spell that."

Ben balled up a napkin and threw it at Sean. He knew Sean was smart, even if his cousin often did his best to hide the evidence.

"Anything new with the guys?" Ben had gotten fond of Sean's three roommates and enjoyed chances to spend time with them. He was equally grateful that they had accepted Erik into the group.

"Darius picked up some swim instructor gigs and part-time life-guarding at a hotel with an indoor pool now that the beach work is done for the season," Sean replied. "Matteo's gotten enough tattoo business that he's raised his rates and still stays busy. And Taylor's bartending. We've been playing through a couple of new video games, and we've beaten all the escape rooms nearby. That's as exciting as we get lately."

"Nothing wrong with that."

Jenny Bladen, Ben's assistant, knocked on the doorframe. "Sorry to interrupt, but housekeeping went to turn over Unit 54, and it doesn't look like Mr. McRaney left on time. He isn't answering the phone or responding to a knock. Do you want to deal with it, or would you like me to handle it?"

Ben gave Sean a knowing look, and Sean grinned. "I'll do it," Ben said. "Since I've got my best bouncer for backup."

They cleaned up the table and headed out to the property, half of a recently remodeled Victorian duplex that kept all its charm despite needed modernizations.

Ben was always surprised at the people who chose to rent off-season, especially as the weather grew colder, ruling out relaxing on the beach. While Cape May never had the frenetic pace of Wildwood, it became positively sedate in the winter months. Community events continued, but were mostly run by and for the locals. With some restaurants and shops closed, familiar faces were seen more often at the places that were still open.

After how impersonal Newark could be, Ben had come to appreciate the small-town vibe Cape May rocked when the tourists went home. He figured the people who chose to spend time here during the quieter months were looking for peace and solitude—or running from something.

"You seriously think the renter is going to be a problem?" Sean asked. He and Ben weren't strangers to knocking on doors and politely reminding people that it was time to go home. For the few who became troublesome, the combination of Ben's sternness and Sean's bodybuilder bulk cut complaints short.

"I hope not. I'm really not in the mood today." Ben dreaded a confrontation.

They reached the unit, and Ben looked around, spotting McRaney's car still in its spot. Drawn curtains over dark windows suggested the man was either out or asleep. He tried once more to call, and they heard the renter's cell phone ringing inside until the call cut off.

Ben rapped on the door. "Rental management. Please open up."

Minutes passed, and Ben couldn't hear any movement inside. He knocked louder with no result.

"Guess we're going in." Ben used his pass key to unlock the door and froze as soon as he stepped over the threshold. He picked up the tang of copper in the air and knew what it meant.

"Management!" he shouted once more for good measure, drawing his gun from the holster at his back.

"Sean—stay outside."

Nothing stirred. Enough light came through the curtains for Ben to see. He cleared the room like he learned in the academy. Ben hoped that perhaps McRaney had merely fallen and knocked himself out, but experience made him prepare for the worst.

Ben peered into the kitchen and felt his gut tighten. McRaney's body lay face down in a pool of blood. Unpleasant experience told Ben from the angle of the gunshot wound that McRaney had been murdered, execution-style.

"Call the police, and don't touch anything!" Ben carefully backed away.

"Why do we need the cops? And why the fuck are you strapped?"

"Just do it," Ben snapped. "He's dead, and it's not self-inflicted."

"Holy Mary, Mother of God." Sean's eyes went wide. He grabbed his phone and dialed 911, giving the address and reported a shooting.

"They're coming," he said as Ben retreated to the porch. "What happened?"

"Dead guy with a double tap," Ben replied. "Someone wanted to make sure McRaney didn't leave Cape May."

"Fuck. You sure?"

Ben gave a curt nod, aware he had automatically gone back into cop mode. "Yeah. Real sure. After you see one...you never forget."

Ben holstered his gun before the Cape May squad car pulled up. He and Sean stood in plain view with their hands raised. Chief Cole Hendricks got out, and his expression shifted from worried to resigned when he saw Ben.

"Figures it would be you, Nolan. And Meirlach. Put your hands down. What the hell is going on?"

"Renter didn't leave on time. Came to see what was going on and found him dead on the floor. Gunshot. Pro-style," Ben recapped.

"Please tell me you didn't contaminate the crime scene."

Ben gave him a look. "Not my first rodeo. I smelled blood when we opened the door and went in thinking he'd gotten hurt. As soon as I saw the body, I backed off. We didn't touch anything except the outside doorknob."

"Why do you always live in interesting times—and drag me into it?" Hendricks muttered. He radioed for an ambulance and the forensic team. "You know any reason why someone would put a hit on your vacationer?"

Ben shook his head. "No idea. Met him once—seemed like a nice old guy. Figured he came for some peace and quiet. I'll pull his paperwork, but given the circumstances, he probably used a fake ID."

"You think?" Hendricks shook his head. "Since you and Mitchell moved here, my life hasn't been boring. And I *liked* boring." He took a deep breath. "I need to handle this. You know the drill. We'll need footage from any surveillance cameras. Come down to the station this afternoon and give your statements. Try not to find any other dead bodies in the meantime."

Ben and Sean walked back to the rental office. Jenny gasped when they told her about McRaney, sparing the details.

"That's awful. I only saw him a couple of times, but he seemed like the gruff but harmless type," she said.

"Since the police are looking into it, please don't say anything," Ben told her. "It definitely wasn't a suicide."

Her eyes widened. "Oh. Do you think it's the Mob?" Jenny dropped her voice to a whisper.

"This is New Jersey. That's always a good place to start," Ben replied. "But the Chief will be pissed if word gets out, and doubly so if there's speculation so..." He mimicked zipping his lips.

Jenny nodded solemnly and repeated the gesture. "Cross my heart."

"Can you please pull any paperwork we have from McRaney? He must have filled out the forms, so there should be something in the files. Bonus if you can find a good photo of him on the security cameras. And put any video on a flash drive for the cops."

"You got it," Jenny replied.

Sean looked at him when Jenny went back to the front desk. "Now what?"

Ben held up a hand while he texted Erik.

Ben: *Found dead guy in one of the rentals. Maybe a Mob hit. No details yet. Be careful. Love you.*

He put his phone down before Erik could reply. "I wanted to warn Erik. This could be completely unrelated to either of us—"

"Yeah, right."

Ben ignored Sean. "But if it isn't, he needs to take precautions."

Sean sobered. "That's why you carry a gun all the time?"

Ben shrugged. "It feels normal to me. And after everything that's happened, I figured better safe than sorry."

"Not exactly the norm for Cape May."

"Neither are Erik and I, apparently. Although we're certainly not the only people who came from somewhere else with a tarnished past."

Sean followed Ben into his office.

"Let's figure out who McRaney really was and why someone wanted him dead," Ben said. "Pull up a chair unless you have somewhere else to be."

Jenny handed off the rental agreement. "I'll go back over the footage and see what I can find. If he wasn't legit he might have tried to avoid the cameras."

Ben pulled up the databases he could access given his private investigator license, which he kept current. "Hendricks won't want to tell us anything, but if we find useful information first, we can pass it to him and maybe get something in exchange," he told Sean after Jenny returned to the front desk.

He entered McRaney's name and address, not surprised when it turned up an old warehouse in Trenton and a long-dead man from Point Pleasant. "Gave us bad info—there's a surprise."

"We could get lucky if Jenny can come up with a photo that's better than his license, and we can get a hit on a facial recognition program," Ben said. "In the meantime, I'll enter his name into the 'known aliases' database and his physical description somewhere else to see if we get any matches. Same with his license plate. Sometimes people slip up and get careless."

"Do you think there's anything in his apartment that might be a clue?" Sean asked, leaning over Ben's shoulder, enthralled.

"There might be, but I don't want to get thrown in jail for

disturbing a crime scene, even if it's my own damn rental unit," Ben replied. "Hendricks has cut us some slack in the past, but goodwill only goes so far. He's basically a good guy, but I think there's a little territory marking going on. You know—small-town cop defending his authority when a big-city hot shot comes to town."

The computer pinged, drawing Ben's attention to the screen. "Okay...we didn't get an exact match on 'Thomas McRaney,' which is the name he rented under. But there's an alias here for a Tom Raines that's pretty close—and the person it's associated with would be about the same age."

"Can you find out anything else?" Sean sounded like he was living out his *NCIS* fantasies.

"Don't get your hopes up," Ben said. "There are a lot of criminals out there."

Ben switched programs yet again and put in the new name. While the search ran, he and Sean got coffee and talked about the weather, the movies playing at the Regent downtown, and which bar had the best wings.

An alert brought them back to the screen. Ben scanned the report. "Apparently Tom Raines was an accountant for the Atlantic City casino Mob in the 1990s," Ben read aloud.

"Doesn't look like he killed anyone or robbed banks, but he probably helped them evade taxes and move money offshore into hidden accounts. Says he disappeared in the early 2000s. No body was found, family eventually declared him legally dead. No one was ever charged with his murder. From the notes, it looks like people either thought he skipped town or got killed by someone who knew how to cover tracks."

Sean sat back in his chair. "That doesn't make sense."

Ben turned to look at him. Sean was intelligent, with sharp street smarts as well. "Why?"

Sean gestured toward the computer with a vague wave of his hand. "So this guy might not do the dirty work, but he knows all the secrets. He'd really have the goods on the Mob—account numbers, banks, dollar amounts. And he had to know they'd come after him if he just vanished—they'd assume he was selling them out to rivals or the feds even if he just wanted to get out of the life."

Ben nodded. "Sounds right."

"You didn't find evidence that he'd testified, so he probably didn't go to the cops," Sean went on. "Though I suppose he could have provided evidence and got moved into Witness Protection. Or maybe he just got scared, figured they'd kill him to shut him up at some point, and decided to make his own retirement plan."

"Maybe."

"Or," Sean continued, barely stopping to take a breath since he was on a roll, "maybe he found out about something and decided to give himself a bonus on the way out. Something that would be sure to tide him over. He plans his escape, sets up what he needs, steals the money, and then leaves his old life behind."

"Ripping off the Mob doesn't usually end well," Ben pointed out.

"Only if they know you did it, and they know what you've taken," Sean countered. "Otherwise, it's friggin' perfect because they can't turn you in."

"They just kill you."

Sean shrugged. "Every plan has its downsides."

By the time Chief Hendricks called for them to give their statements two hours later, Ben had compiled a fairly thorough profile of Tom Raines even without access to police records.

"Are you going to share that with the cops?" Sean asked as they walked to the police station.

"I'm going to *trade* it for more information," Ben replied. "Cole knows that if he doesn't fill me in more than he might with a regular civilian, I'll just call in favors to get what I want. We've done this dance before."

Hendricks was waiting for them and ushered them into a conference room. He was close to Ben's age and height, with short, sandy brown hair and brown eyes. By this point in the day, reddish stubble shaded his jawline. Hendricks read off the usual disclaimer about their statements being recorded and had them state their names and addresses.

"Tell me what happened," Hendricks said when the preliminaries were out of the way.

"Exactly what we said when you got to the rental unit," Ben replied. "The renter had overstayed his reservation, and Jenny asked me to let him know."

"Why you?"

Ben shrugged. "Most folks are pretty nice, but we've had one or two get unpleasant when they are trying to eke out an extra half day without paying. They're likely to give me fewer problems than they do her."

"Was there a reason you felt threatened enough to take a body-guard?" Hendricks asked with a glance at Sean.

Ben and Sean both chuckled. "Old habit and we were together when Jenny called me. Sean and I worked at the rental company for his parents—my aunt and uncle—all the time we were growing up. The nice people weren't a problem. The rude people were nicer when there were two of us—especially after Sean started lifting weights."

"And your concealed carry?" Hendricks raised an eyebrow. Ben met his gaze.

"I have a permit. The gun is legal. You know what the past year's been like. I intended to give up carrying when I moved here and then reconsidered, given everything."

Hendricks grimaced. "Can't say I fault you on that. Walk me through, step by step."

Ben and Sean recounted what they saw, repeating what they had reported at the site.

"What made you draw your weapon?" Hendricks asked, more intrigued than accusatory.

"Old habit. Gut feeling. I smelled blood," Ben said. "I was hoping the guy had a bad fall, but something just felt *off*. I called out and no one answered. When I saw the body—from a distance—I backed out, and Sean called it in."

"Was there anything before today that made you wonder about Mr. McRaney?"

"If I'd have thought he was trouble up front, we would have

declined him," Ben replied. "There weren't any red flags. But in hindsight..." He pulled out the folder with a copy of the results of his recent sleuthing.

"The old guy wasn't as harmless as he looked. We think he was Tom Raines, Mob accountant and long-time missing person," Ben said with a bit of a smirk as he handed off the folder. "You can probably validate that if you run his prints."

"I'm not going to ask how you got this." Hendricks looked like he might be getting a headache.

"All completely legal sources for a licensed private eye and someone with good Google-fu," Ben replied. "I take anything that could be a threat to Erik's and my safety very seriously," he said, humor fading. "We both thought we got out of the Mob's sights when we moved here, but you know better than anyone that didn't happen."

"Not every mobster on the Jersey Shore is after you, Nolan," Hendricks said.

"Sure feels like it."

"Are you going to let us do our job investigating this? Unless you have a tip, and then you report it like a good citizen *who does not take the law into his own hands?*"

"There's no law against armchair sleuthing," Ben countered. "I know for a fact you don't have a homicide detective on staff. Although the way things are going, maybe you should put that in the budget."

"Very funny."

"I'm just saying that as long as I stay in my lane, I've got skills your staff is thin on," Ben said. "And I'm not a civvie. Had the badge; got my license."

"Do you have any reason to think McRaney—or Raines, if that's who he turns out to be—had any connection to the cases you or Mitchell handled?"

Ben took it as a positive that Hendricks hadn't shot his proposal down right out of the gate. "No. At least, not yet. And I'll be glad if nothing shows up. But considering our history, I'd rather not make assumptions."

Hendricks looked like he was fighting down an upset stomach.

Ben bet the chief was weighing his options. "If you stick to authorized, legitimate sources...and you don't interfere with our investigation...I can't stop you from being an 'armchair detective,'" he finally said. "But...step outside those lines, and I will take action. Am I clear?"

"Crystal," Ben replied. It was better than he had hoped, and while he counted Hendricks as an ally, he still felt like their interactions often turned into pissing matches.

"Then get out of here. If you find anything that's pertinent to the case, I expect you to let me know."

"And if you discover that McRaney is somehow tangled up with something from my past or Erik's, I'm trusting you to warn us," Ben returned in a level voice.

"*If* it turns out that something about the case might put either of you in danger, I will certainly alert you," Hendricks said. "And that's subject to my judgment."

Ben nodded with a straight face, but he figured that Hendricks also knew that his mother—Erik's friend Susan—would never let him hear the last of it otherwise.

"Deal," Ben agreed as he and Sean got up to leave.

"And if you've got your food truck with you, make sure you've got all the permits," Hendricks called as they headed out. Sean shot him a thumbs-up.

"Well, at least you used the correct finger," Ben said once they were outside. "The one that didn't get us arrested."

"And people doubt my intelligence," Sean scoffed. "What now?"

Ben glanced at his phone, which he had silenced while he was at the police station. The string of texts and voice messages from Erik made his next steps clear.

"I need to fill Erik in on what's going on before he makes me sleep on the couch," Ben replied. "Go see your friends and do whatever else you wanted to do while you're here. Do you need to stay in one of the rentals? We have a lot of vacancies."

"That works for me." Sean followed Ben back to the office and Ben handed off a set of keys.

"I don't think anyone will bother you, but considering what happened...just keep your eyes open," Ben warned.

"I always do," Sean assured him with a jaunty, mocking salute as he headed for his car.

Ben checked in with Jenny, made sure there wasn't anything that demanded his attention, and then poured himself a hot cup of coffee before he closed his office door and settled in at his desk. He hesitated before he pressed the call button.

I know Erik has his own baggage and made some enemies, but I hate the idea that my crappy past is going to put him in danger.

He'd say the same thing, and if he did, I'd assure him that I love him too much to care. I want to keep him safe. But when it's my past causing the problems, I feel responsible. I don't want him to get hurt. I can't imagine losing him. I just hope he doesn't wake up one day and decide that I'm too broken to be worth the effort.

We didn't need more ghosts from the past on top of getting settled in together. It's like we can't catch a break. But I want this thing between us more than I think I've ever wanted anything in my life.

Aunt Meg always said that what was worth having was worth fighting for, so I'm fighting hard as fuck for Erik.

Erik picked up on the second ring. "Ben—what's going on? Six people have already called to tell me about the police and an ambulance at one of your rentals. On top of your text about a dead guy."

Ben could hear the strain from Erik trying to remain calm, as well as the undercurrent of anxiety worrying about Ben's safety and fearing another surprise from his own past.

"Right now, that's all we've got—a dead guy," Ben told him. "Except he didn't do the deed himself, and whoever offed him was a pro. I did some digging and I think he might have been here under an alias—someone who disappeared twenty years ago and probably knew a dangerous amount about the Mob's business."

"Fuck," Erik swore. "Please tell me that he isn't someone you investigated—or someone I testified against."

"Doesn't seem likely," Ben replied. "He would have been in hiding by the time we were doing our jobs. I'm chasing down leads from my sources. And, get this—I talked Hendricks into not ragging on my ass for researching as long as I don't get in his way."

"Obviously Susan has put in a good word for us," Erik snarked.

"Never underestimate the ability of a mother to pull strings," Ben said. "I'm glad she's on our side."

"Do you think the dead guy has anything to do with the poker chips or Fun Factory?"

Ben had expected the question. "I don't have any reason to—yet. They'd both be before his time. The only link might be that he worked for the Mob in Atlantic City, but we don't know that the mafia had anything to do with Fun Factory. Sewell Point sounds penny-ante compared to the real action on the Boardwalk."

"I'm going to see Jaxon later this afternoon, so I'll let you know whether he has any intel." Erik sounded somewhat mollified, and Ben felt relieved that Erik wasn't angry at not getting a call sooner.

"And I'll keep working my sources," Ben promised. "What I can't access, I'm betting that Vic D'Amato can." Vic was a friend and a homicide detective in Myrtle Beach who also hunted supernatural killers. He already had an email drafted to send to Vic, and he was adding to it as he thought of more questions.

"Did you get any sense that the dead guy's ghost hung around? Maybe he'd like to spill his guts before he moves on to his eternal reward."

"I don't think he'd been dead very long. Couple of hours at most. Some ghosts take longer than that to realize they've croaked," Ben replied. "Maybe Monty can stage an intervention."

Monty Clark ran the Cape May lighthouse. In addition to being a park ranger, he was a powerful medium, although he didn't publicize his talent.

"I'll call Monty and see if he's willing to try to talk to the ghost," Ben said.

"Are you okay?"

Ben sighed. "There's no reason to think right now that we're not safe, so I'm okay as far as that goes. The dead guy in a rental unit means paperwork, special clean-up, and an insurance claim, so it'll be a hassle. I just wish the past would stay in the past."

"How's Sean?"

"Living large and taking names," Ben replied. "I'll tell you all about it tonight. Have fun with Jaxon."

"Love you. Stay safe."

"You too." Ben ended the call and leaned back in his chair, closing his eyes for a moment and hoping to fend off a stress headache.

Hendricks is right—Erik and I didn't piss off the entire East Coast Mob. McRaney—Raines—could have picked my rentals completely by coincidence. It doesn't mean anyone is coming after Erik and me.

So why does my gut say different?

FOUR

ERIK

"Is Etta Campbell in?" Erik asked at the library's front desk.

The receptionist looked up. "May I tell her your name?"

"Erik Mitchell. Susan Hendricks and Ben Nolan—Meg Meirlach's nephew—sent me."

That brought a smile. "Any friend of theirs is a friend of mine. Give me a moment and I'll go get Etta."

Erik didn't have long to wait before an older woman with short blond hair and bright blue eyes strode toward him. She wore a colorful sweater over a blouse and slacks. A pair of reading glasses dangled from a chain made from multi-hued crystals.

"Etta Campbell." She offered her hand and gave a firm shake. "How do you know Ben and Susan?"

"Ben Nolan is my partner," Erik replied, pleased when his answer didn't even get a blink in response. "And Susan is my next-door neighbor."

"Wonderful. What brings you here, and how can I help?"

"I'm the new owner at Trinkets, and someone mailed us an envelope full of old poker chips from a place called the Fun Factory. I'm not finding much information except that it might have been early in the 1900s and was possibly located in Sewell Point."

Etta frowned, thinking. "That name rings a bell, but I can't come up with details off-hand. Let's check it out."

He followed her into the back area of the reference section. "This is where we put the stuff that isn't very sexy," Etta said with a laugh. "Government records and reports, old newspapers, that sort of thing. It's not casual browsing material."

She waved toward a wooden table. "Go on, have a seat. Let me see what I can scrounge up."

Erik read the news on his phone to keep from drumming his fingers or fidgeting in his chair. Ben's news worried him more than he let on, and he dreaded having to watch over their shoulders once more.

Etta was back before he'd finished with the latest headlines. She had a stack of books and binders, which she set on the table with a solid thump.

"That far back, most of it isn't digitized because, well, there's just not much demand." She sat across the table from Erik. "I actually had to dust these off. But if your Fun Factory existed, we should find a record somewhere in here."

"We know it was before 1930 because of the type of poker chip," Erik volunteered. "And it's just a hunch, but I'm going to bet we should start by looking between 1908 to 1918."

"That's very specific." Etta peered at him over her reading glasses. "Can I ask why those years?"

Erik sighed. "Those would have been the first years of the Commodore Wilson. It's a long story, but I swear everything in my life seems to come back to that hotel."

She raised an eyebrow. "You're rather young to be haunted by a hotel that shut down when you were a kid."

"It's complicated." Erik decided to shift the topic. "What are we looking for in the books?"

"Assuming the Fun Factory was a legitimate public business, there should be tax records," Etta told him. "That's the first thing. After that, when we've got the dates nailed down, we might find newspaper articles or legal filings."

She handed an old binder of reports to Erik and took one for herself. "You've got 1908, and I've got 1909. I brought out 1900 to 1910. If we don't find anything in these, I can get the next few."

They scanned the yellowed pages, working silently. Erik didn't find anything in his volume and reached for the 1910 report.

"Bingo," Etta murmured a few minutes later. "Take a look at this." She turned her book for Erik to see, and he followed the line her finger traced.

"Fun Factory, entertainment venue, Sewell's Point," he read aloud, excited to find confirmation. "Jepson Enterprises."

"Jepson," Etta repeated. "Now that name I've heard—and I think there's a link with the Commodore Wilson." She took the other books back with her into the stacks and returned shortly with several new volumes.

"I did a quick online search to confirm my hunch." She placed her phone on the table. "Nathan Jepson was the second owner of the Commodore Wilson. He bought it from Howard Caine, the man who built the hotel and envisioned making Cape May the new Nantucket." She gave a wry chuckle. "It didn't quite work out that way."

"Jepson must have had money, even if he bought the hotel when it was distressed," Erik commented.

"He made it—and lost it," Etta confirmed. She opened another thick book and searched for the right page. "This is a history of Cape May in the same period. Jepson warranted inclusion as a real estate mogul. He made a lot of money building hotels and restaurants along the railroad lines to encourage people to travel. Then he sank most of what he had in the Commodore Wilson and, like all the other owners, couldn't make a go of it."

Erik did not mention the site's malicious genius loci as the probable reason for the hotel's ruination. "So Jepson owned both the hotel and Fun Factory?"

Etta ran her finger down the columns of small type in the old book. "Here we go."

Erik leaned forward to see.

"There's not much, but it's a note about a new theater, arcade, and casino on the Sewell's Point pier called the Fun Factory," she noted. "And there's an address."

They found entries in the books for 1910 through 1914, then nothing.

"Uh-oh," Etta said. "That's not good. A lot of places had catastrophic fires back in the day. Or the owner just went bankrupt."

Searching the newspaper microfiche for 1914 turned up one headline. "Sewell's Point casino destroyed by fire," Erik read aloud. He skimmed down through the article.

"According to this, it had a vaudeville theater, arcade, bowling alley, and casino," Erik continued. "And it says 'fire of uncertain origin.' Hmm…do you think that's code for 'Atlantic City Mob didn't like the competition'?"

Etta smirked. "That's always a possibility. Or 'owner needed the insurance money.' Well, you found what you were looking for."

Erik snapped pictures of the documents with his phone before helping Etta put everything back. "Thank you so much. You have some great resources. I'm sure I'll be back."

"Please visit again. And I'll have to poke my nose into your shop. Susan's been after me to drop by, and I just never seem to find the time," Etta replied.

Erik checked his watch when he left the library and realized enough time had passed to catch up to Jaxon at the end of his day at the Center for the Arts.

He drove over and parked next to the building. The sign outside announced "Jersey Shore Amusements: A History of Fun in the Sun."

The receptionist smiled when he walked in and waved him through. "Mr. Davies is expecting you."

Erik found Jaxon in the main exhibit room, overseeing the placement of cases and signage.

"Erik! Great timing. I was just finishing here. Come see what we're working on, and then we can go back to my office."

Jaxon Davies still had the stage presence honed by decades on Broadway and his charisma magic. Tall, slender, with bleached white hair and an eclectic fashion sense, he reminded Erik of David Bowie in the singer's "Thin White Duke" era.

"Amusement parks?" Erik walked into the jumble of a display in progress.

"Don't mind the mess—it's truly organized chaos." Jaxon dismissed the litter of packing crates and half-assembled displays.

"How is it that whenever you do an exhibit, the theme ends up haunting me in real life?"

Jaxon turned, intrigued. "Do tell. What now?"

"Does your exhibit have anything about the Fun Factory in Sewell's Point?"

Jaxon's eyes widened. "We do. Erik—you've got to tell me everything."

Erik pulled out his phone and scrolled to the photo of the old poker chips. "These arrived in the mail without a return address. They're a little haunted, and I think the owner came to a bad end."

Jaxon took the phone and made the image larger. "You wouldn't consider lending them to us for the display, would you?"

"Did you miss the part about 'a little haunted'?" Erik teased. "If we can figure out where they came from and make sure there's nothing dangerous hanging around, I'm happy to lend them. What do you know?"

Jaxon took him by the elbow and guided Erik to a corner of the room. "This is our 'Paradise Lost' part of the exhibit—a tribute to the parks that have disappeared over the years."

One of the displays featured a map and a legend of the places marked, each of them a now-defunct amusement park with the dates of operation.

"Wow. I knew New Jersey had been a tourist spot for a long time, but these go back to the 1800s," Erik said, fascinated. "I'll admit that I'm a sucker for a good theme park even though I'm not a coaster fan."

"Get your boy to take you to Wildwood more often," Jaxon said with a knowing wink. "Ride the rides, eat junk food, and make out on the Ferris wheel."

"Is Arjun a fan?" Erik teased back, mentioning Jaxon's husband.

"I'll never tell." Jaxon struck a campy pose.

Erik sobered. "Here it is. Fun Factory." He traced the name with his finger. "It only lasted a few years."

"We have a photo of one tower, which is the only thing left from the old days," Jaxon replied. "There's a military base on the land now. It wasn't really like Palisades Park or Luna Park. Never had rides, and it wasn't at the end of a railway line."

Jaxon grew more animated as he warmed to the subject. "It was more like the early version of the sort of entertainment nexus you'd find in a Vegas hotel today. It had a restaurant, arcade games like Skee Ball and the sort you'd find on a carnival midway, plus a bowling alley. Since it was on a pier, in the summer there was the beach and boating."

"I found an old article that mentioned a theater and a casino," Erik added.

Jaxon nodded enthusiastically. "Yes. The theater had vaudeville performances, plays, and early motion pictures. The casino even had a few slot machines, although it was mostly card and dice games. It really was a one-stop date night kind of place. Very exciting for the time—and a bit more in keeping with the Cape May atmosphere than Wildwood."

"Any good salacious stories?" Erik prompted. "Famous murders? Mafia hits? Celebrity scandals?"

Jaxon gave him a look. "Are you expecting trouble?"

"It seems to find me whether I'm expecting it or not," Erik replied. "The impression I got from the poker chips is that their owner met a bad end. Murdered, probably shot." Jaxon knew about Erik's touch magic, and had helped them piece together evidence before.

"Fun Factory wasn't as showy as Luna Park and some of the others. They were dripping with electric lights and had all the latest and greatest attractions. Still, if there's gambling, someone usually has their fingers in the pie, and the Jersey Shore was a hotbed in those years. There was even a television show about the Atlantic City Mob back in the day that revived interest in the history."

"Interesting," Erik said. "And by the way, before you ask, I'm not picking up bad vibes from anything in the room. If there are ghosts, they're not showing themselves, and I don't think they're strong enough to cause trouble."

"Thank you." Jaxon put a hand over his chest in relief. "I don't want to explain to the insurance company that someone had a heart attack because a ghost jumped out of our exhibit."

"I don't think you need to worry about that." Erik chuckled. "I can't wait to see how this all comes together. If you find out anything else about the Fun Factory, let me know. I have a gut feeling it's going to turn out to be important."

"You and Ben need to come for dinner again soon," Jaxon said as he walked out of the display room with Erik. They went to his office, and Jaxon made Nespresso lattes for both of them before settling onto the sofa facing Erik.

"Did Ben finish moving in? How's the love nest?" Jaxon joked.

"Yes, he moved in, and we've got things pretty well pulled together, at least for now," Erik said. "I didn't realize how much I'd started to be a set-in-my-ways confirmed bachelor until it came to rearranging furniture and swapping artwork."

Jaxon smiled as he sipped his drink. "You should have seen Arjun and me in our first apartment. All of his video game art and my theater posters."

Arjun Chandramohan made a fortune from the software company he founded before cashing in and retiring in his forties. Erik suspected that their "first apartment" was more of a penthouse.

"It's a strange feeling, making room in your space for someone else," Erik mused. "I'm thrilled that Ben agreed to move in. I'm head over heels for the guy."

"Obviously."

"But it's still an adjustment having to account for another person in everything. When I lived with someone before, I traveled so much of the time, I don't think we spent enough time in the same space to ever have to compromise," Erik said, realizing that for the first time.

"Sounds like when Arjun and I got together. We were both instantly smitten—truly love at first sight—but we'd both been on our own for a long time. He was just getting ready to leave the company behind, and building it had been all-consuming. And I was still on Broadway, which is not a nine-to-five job," Jaxon replied. "We had to decide that the relationship was the priority before we could even begin to worry about picking out curtains or throw pillows," he added with a laugh.

"Did it go smoothly?" Erik and Ben hadn't had any serious disagreements, but his old boyfriend had a tendency to act out, something Erik understood more in hindsight.

"Oh my," Jaxon said. "You've met us, right? I'm dramatic, and Arjun is intense. Combustible sex doesn't make up for leaving socks and damp towels on the floor!"

"TMI!" Erik laughed.

"Yes, darling. We had to work at it. There were snits and silences and theatrical exits and slamming doors, and then we grew up." Jaxon let out a long breath. "And we realized that if we wanted to keep what we had, I had to put in the energy that I gave to my roles, and he had to commit like he did developing a program. I think that led both of us to step away from what we'd been doing a few years before we would have otherwise."

Erik nodded, hiding behind his latte for a few moments while he let that sink in. "I know I don't want a relationship like my parents have. They're consumed with the social scene and impressing the neighbors. Ben definitely doesn't want to repeat how he grew up. But none of the couples in the sitcoms I watched as a kid looked like us."

Jaxon set his empty cup aside. "That's where I had an advantage in the theater. There were plenty of gay men and lots of couples. It was easy to watch and learn about what you could have, what you wanted and didn't want. And while there were always people who changed partners like underwear, it was the ones who didn't that stuck with me. Those older couples—I knew I wanted that." He sighed. "And I'm lucky enough to have gotten my wish."

"Thank you," Erik said. "You've been exactly what I needed today."

A reminder chimed on Jaxon's phone. "I'm afraid duty calls. I'm glad you came by. Tell Ben 'hi' for me, and I meant what I said about dinner once this exhibit gets pulled together."

Jaxon walked Erik back to the front entrance, chatting about the weather. Just as they reached the door, Jaxon put a hand on Erik's arm.

"If either of you need anything, just call. I mean it."

Erik smiled. "I know you do, and we appreciate it."

His thoughts whirled as he drove back to Trinkets. He wondered whether Ben or the cops had turned up more information about the dead man and how—or if—there was a connection to the poker chips or something in his or Ben's past.

"Find out anything?" Susan asked when he got to the shop.

The store was temporarily empty, so Erik filled her in on what he had learned.

"That's a lot for a handful of old poker chips," she said. "Do you think there's any connection to the body Ben found?"

Erik wasn't sure whether Susan kept a police scanner handy or just benefited from being the mother of the chief of police, but she always seemed to know what was going on.

"I hope not, but the way things seem to go for us, there's probably something," he admitted. "And we'll find out when it bites us on the butt."

The rest of the afternoon was uneventful, to Erik's relief. He filled orders from the website while Susan took care of the handful of customers who drifted in to browse.

"Have a good evening," he told Susan as they locked up.

"If you and Ben need anything, just let me know," Susan replied, a standing offer that Erik deeply appreciated.

"I think I just need a nap," Erik said. "I've had a headache since I got back from Jaxon's."

She checked her watch. "If you lie down right now, you might get some shuteye before Ben gets home. Sometimes fifteen minutes can do a world of good."

He thanked her and climbed the stairs, promising himself Advil when he reached the kitchen. After swallowing a couple of tablets,

Erik stretched out on the couch and pulled a throw blanket over himself.

Erik tried to relax and ignore the throbbing pain in his temples. He slowed his breathing and did his best to let go of the tension he felt in his neck and shoulders. After a bit, the pills kicked in, and the headache eased as he drifted off.

He found himself in the hallway outside his old apartment in Atlanta, the one he shared with Josh. His carry-on suitcase hugged his leg, and Erik moved his messenger bag out of the way as he reached for his keys. This last trip to Belgium had taken more out of him than he expected, and he had been happy for the chance to come home early.

Erik planned to freshen up and order dinner to surprise Josh when he got home from work. He'd missed his boyfriend. Constant travel wore on both of them, and Erik wanted to make it up to him.

His key turned in the lock, and he opened the door, then froze at the thumping noise he heard. Erik left his bags in the kitchen and pulled his phone from his pocket, ready to call the police if he had interrupted a robbery.

Moving silently, Erik entered the dining room—and saw two naked figures bent over the dining room table. Josh's hips pumped as he fucked the man beneath him—Erik's assistant, Lee.

Erik's heart sped dangerously fast, and he felt the beginning of a panic attack rise.

"Get out!" he roared, and the two men uncoupled gracelessly.

"Erik—it isn't..." Josh started.

"It absolutely is," Erik yelled. "Get your pants and get out." He looked at Lee. "You're fired." His attention returned to Josh, who didn't even look ashamed. "You don't live here anymore."

"You can't—" Josh protested.

"I totally can. My apartment. My lease. Now get the fuck out of here."

Josh kept trying to argue, and Erik focused on breathing.

"Out!" he yelled to shut Josh up. Lee had already covered himself and fled.

"What did you expect when you're never home?" Josh spat as he hurried into his clothes. "Did you think I'd wait forever? Lee's more fun in the sack than you ever were."

Erik picked up the closest thing at hand, a vase, and threw it down next to Josh. It practically exploded on the wood floor.

"I won't miss next time," he vowed and picked up a decorative globe from the sideboard.

Josh raised his hands in a gesture of surrender and started to back toward the door. "Okay, okay. Geez. It was just fucking."

"Leave now, and I won't burn your stuff." Erik didn't recognize his own voice.

"Holy shit. You've lost your mind."

Erik raised the orb to throw. He didn't pitch softball, but at this distance he couldn't miss.

"I'm going!" Josh hurried to the door without buttoning his shirt or buckling his belt. He paused in the opening. "Screw me over and you'll be sorry. I've got friends who are lawyers. I can sue your ass for everything you've got."

"My friends are Interpol," Erik said in a cold, hard tone. "They can make you disappear."

Josh's eyes went wide as if he finally realized he'd gone too far. He backed out of the door, and Erik slammed it behind him.

Erik collapsed to his knees, heaving for breath as the world swam around him. He hadn't had a major panic attack since shortly after his shooting, but he remembered the lead-up clearly. Erik fell back on his ass, leaning against the cabinets and closed his eyes, just trying not to pass out.

"Fuck, fuck, fuck, fuck." Later, when the anger cooled, he'd feel the heartbreak. But right now everything twisted up together inside. His heart pounded, and he swore bands were tightening around his chest, suffocating him. Erik couldn't stifle a moan. He lurched to one side and threw up, then crawled away and curled in a ball, shaking so hard his teeth chattered.

"Erik." The voice came from far away. *Not Josh.*

"Erik, wake up." The speaker sounded concerned, even fearful. Erik couldn't concentrate, didn't want anyone nearby, and definitely didn't want to be touched. He panicked when he couldn't move his legs.

"Whoa. Hold steady—you're tangled up in the throw. Don't kick me or put a hole in it."

Seconds later, his feet were free, and Erik swallowed hard, trying not to retch.

"Erik, love, whatever's going on in your head isn't real. Come back. Please, babe. Open your eyes."

Erik still gasped for air, but he forced himself to open his eyes. It took a few seconds to recognize the worried face inches from his own.

"Ben?"

Ben slumped with relief. "Oh, thank God. You scared the shit out of me. Panic attack?"

The awful fog of memories started to clear. Ben moved toward him slowly like Erik was a spooked horse and finally enfolded him in an embrace that was close enough to reassure but didn't trap him.

"Christ, you're cold as ice," Ben fretted, running his palms up and down Erik's arms. "Listen to my heartbeat, and breathe with me. In. Out. I've got you. I won't let go. I'm here. Just hang onto me and breathe. In. Out."

Erik focused on Ben's voice, the warmth of his body, the strength of his hands. His stomach stopped pitching, and gradually his heart quit pounding.

"It's okay, you're safe," Ben whispered over and over.

Finally, Erik stilled. Ben didn't let go.

"Want to talk about it?"

Erik didn't, but he knew Ben deserved an answer. *God, I'm so broken. I don't know why he sticks around.*

"Bad dream," Erik managed.

"The shooting?" Ben's voice was low and steady, but Erik heard the concern and, beneath it, affection.

Erik shook his head. "That day—"

"Shh," Ben soothed, and Erik knew his partner understood his meaning. "That's long over. It's just us now. You're out of that life, far away. Just us," he repeated, holding Erik close.

"I'm sorry," Erik whispered.

"Nothing to be sorry about, babe," Ben assured him, his voice a comforting rumble.

"I'm a mess." At least Erik hadn't thrown up for real. He hoped.

"Have you seen me? I come with a whole matched set of psychological baggage," Ben replied, trying to lighten the mood. "We can be messes together."

Eventually Erik pulled away and Ben eased his grip. He ran a hand back through sweat-soaked hair and realized his shirt clung to his skin. "I need a shower."

Ben's fingers gently stroked his cheek. Erik closed his eyes and let himself lean into the touch. "How about you make sure you're steady before that, huh? Don't want to scrape you off the tile."

Erik nodded. "Sorry."

"I don't like to see you hurting, but there's no apology necessary. Two steps forward, one step back," Ben said. "At least that's what my mandated psych counselor told me after I got shot."

They sat together in silence for several more minutes before Erik felt reasonably confident that he could stand without falling over. Ben didn't move when Erik stood, but Erik could see that his partner had tensed to catch him if necessary.

"I think I'm okay," Erik rasped.

"How about I go fix you a cup of tea with plenty of sugar and maybe some crackers or cookies," Ben suggested. "It'll settle your stomach."

Erik nodded. "Sounds good."

He made it to the bathroom, although he still felt lightheaded. His breathing and pulse were slower but hadn't gone back yet to normal. Erik kept his thoughts blank as he stripped off his clothes and turned on the shower, running the water hot.

Erik leaned on the sink and stared at the stranger in the mirror. He met his haunted gaze, holding onto the cold porcelain with a death grip.

I'm in Cape May, not Atlanta. Josh is history. Ben loves me. Things are good. Now I just need to not fuck it up.

He got into the shower and let the hot water warm him, driving away the shakes. The eucalyptus-scented soap calmed his nerves.

Erik ran through the grounding mantras he had learned from his stint in therapy and gradually felt the last tendrils of the nightmare slip free, leaving him exhausted physically and mentally.

He got out when the water cooled, toweled off, and dressed slowly. Erik realized he was dragging his feet, ashamed that Ben had seen his meltdown. He knew his partner wouldn't judge him, but Erik hated to show the damaged side of himself, especially since their relationship was still so new.

On the other hand, good for him to know what he's really getting into. If he doesn't want to deal with it, sooner is better than later to find that out.

As promised, Ben had tea and cookies waiting in the kitchen. "Sit. Eat." Ben motioned Erik to the table.

"I'm—"

"Don't you dare apologize again." Ben's voice was gentle. "You have every right to work through your shit at your own pace. What happened, happened. I'm glad I was here in time to help. Please don't think you have to hide anything from me. I love you."

Erik looked down, feeling his cheeks color. "I love you too. So much. Thank you. It's just…I feel like there've been scarier things to have PTSD over than a cheating boyfriend, you know?"

Ben shrugged. "We don't get to pick."

Erik sighed. "I guess you're right. But, Christ, Josh wasn't worth it, and it pisses me off that he left me with a scar that won't heal." Erik intentionally eased his grip on the mug to keep from snapping off the handle.

"Hasn't healed—*yet*," Ben corrected gently. "It will. Scars fade."

Erik reached out and took hold of Ben's hand. He kissed Ben's knuckles. "I don't deserve you." That skirted dangerously close to the thoughts that haunted him.

Ben tipped Erik's face up so that their eyes met. "Stop that. You're amazing. I'm lucky to have you. We're both a bit dented, so we'll have to cover for each other. That's all. There's no one I'd rather be with, and I mean that with all my heart."

Erik knew that his tough Jersey cop boyfriend didn't bare his heart easily. *I must have really scared him.*

"Okay." Erik knew better than to argue, even though his demons weren't fully silenced.

"How about we order in and then curl up and watch movies?" Ben suggested. "Put everything else out of mind for tonight."

Erik knew he should probably be more worried about the ominous connections between Fun Factory and the Commodore Wilson, but right now he couldn't muster the energy.

"Sounds like a plan," he said with a grateful smile.

"Don't stress. Let me take care of you. It'll be okay," Ben assured.

Every time Erik thought it wasn't possible to fall more in love with his partner, Ben did something that proved him wrong. It had been difficult to get over Josh's betrayal and trust again, but deep down, Erik knew that cheating wasn't in Ben's personality. *And I had warning signs I ignored about Josh.*

Ben and I have fought and nearly died for each other. I know what we have is real. Now I just have to keep my damage from getting in my way.

"Go get comfortable. I'll order online and be right in," Ben told him. "Pick the movie. Whatever you choose will be fine with me."

Erik chose one of their favorite action movies and headed back to the couch, where he wrapped himself in the knitted throw and waited for Ben to join him.

Moments later, Ben took his seat and pulled the blanket over them, then slung an arm around Erik's shoulders. "I got us Chinese food, ordered your favorite stuff. Let's watch things blow up and forget about everything else."

Erik leaned his head against Ben's shoulder and smiled.

FIVE

BEN

"I'm here in an unofficial capacity," Chief Hendricks said when he sat in the chair across from Ben's desk at the real estate office. "Consider it a friendly update."

"I appreciate that," Ben replied. "What's up?"

"Turns out your dead renter, Tom Raines, came from a minor crime family of his own," Hendricks said. "They were lieutenants, not bosses, but he had a number of relatives in the Mob, including his father and several cousins. Not all of them had desk jobs like Raines."

Ben hadn't had a chance to look that deeply into Raines's history. Now his thoughts spun, trying to figure out where the connections might have been.

"Two of his cousins worked for honchos in the Seventh Avenue gang that you helped bust," Hendricks said. "His father, Galen, was a suspect in several high-profile robberies back in the 1960s but never faced charges. Notes on the case suggest that someone called in favors to have the investigation mismanaged."

"Sounds like the Newark I left behind," Ben noted. "Did you follow the money? It's always about the cash."

Hendricks nodded. "I wasn't born yesterday, Nolan. Although

before you and Mitchell moved to Cape May, most of my Mob exposure was at the movies."

"Galen wasn't the only thief in the family," Hendricks continued. "His father, Edwin, stole all of a casino's money the same night the casino burned. He hid the stash before his enemies killed him, but no one ever found the loot. Rumor had it that Galen spent his whole life searching for the treasure, without luck, and that he was killed by mobsters who thought he knew where it was."

"Talk about lousy luck," Ben replied.

"Yeah, well the apple didn't fall far from the tree. Tom Raines used what he knew as a Mob accountant to embezzle a small fortune, and then skipped town, managing to hide for two decades before he came back to Cape May and promptly got killed," Hendricks said.

"Does that mean you've got a lead about who killed him? Did they think he still had the money after all that time?" Ben asked.

"No leads yet. Enough years have gone by now that most of the perps and the detectives on the case are dead or too old to remember details," Hendricks answered.

"We count on crooks being in a hurry to become big spenders. If they go out and pay cash for a mansion and a boat and a fancy car when they were barely making the payments on a crappy used car, that's like sending up a flare. Otherwise, it gets harder. After a while, I imagine the department put its resources elsewhere, and the Mob bided its time," he added.

"But why would Tom come back at all when he'd gotten away? Unless...do you think he had a lead on his grandfather's hidden treasure?"

"Maybe. Or someone thought he did."

"He was a Mob accountant. Tom probably knew a lot of stuff that his bosses wanted to keep on the down low," Ben pointed out. "He did better at disappearing than WITSEC usually manages. Whatever pulled him out of hiding had to be pretty damn compelling. He had to know the Mob has a long memory."

Hendricks's expression darkened. "I don't like this, Nolan. At the very least, we've got a contract killer in my territory. And if other people think that Raines knew where Edwin's treasure was and left clues behind, this could get more dangerous."

"Do you need something from me? Because you didn't have to fill me in," Ben replied.

"I thought you should know what we found, since Raines's cousins and his dad were involved with the Newark Mob. Raines himself had closer ties to the Atlantic City families," Hendricks said. "Just in case that either suggested ideas to you about who killed him or warned you about who might be involved."

"I appreciate that. Let me see what I can find out—discreetly," Ben said. "Because if there's a connection to any of my old cases, it's likely to show up in the worst possible way."

"I'm trusting you not to overplay your hand on this, Nolan," Hendricks warned. "Remember where the line is between who you are and who you used to be."

"I'm even more eager to shut those doors than you are," Ben assured him. "I came to Cape May to start over. But I can't do that if there are still hot links to the Mob—they might bide their time, but they never forget."

"You want to protect Erik. I want to protect the town. That's why I would appreciate your help—unofficially, of course," Hendricks added with a lopsided smirk.

"Of course. Thank you." With all the mayhem that seemed to follow Ben and Erik to Cape May, Hendricks would be within his rights to dislike them both. While they still occasionally sparred and Ben remained convinced the chief of police needed to assert dominance, the relationship was much better than it could have been.

"Try not to touch off another Mob war," Hendricks said as he rose to leave. "We've only just gotten the bullet holes out of the squad cars from the last time."

"I'll do my best."

Jenny hurried in after Hendricks left. "Did he have news about the dead guy?"

Ben appreciated Jenny's help and her loyalty but feared the juicy gossip potential might overcome her willpower. "I'll fill you in when I can," he told her. "I don't want to put you in danger, and honestly, we don't exactly know what's going on."

"Thanks for the chivalry, but don't cut me out of the action," Jenny said with a no-nonsense look. "Besides, I've got a lead. I think our dead guy spent at least some of his time in Maine."

Ben frowned, surprised. "Maine?"

"The police released the crime scene, and I went in to see what needed to be packed up before we get the specialty cleaners, in case there's next of kin," Jenny said. "I was checking the nightstand, and I happened to see something under one of the pillows on the bed. It was a very handsome custom-made knife. Made and sold only by a blade-smith in Maine."

"He could have picked it up on vacation," Ben replied.

"It's a numbered limited edition," Jenny continued. "So no matter when he got it, the bladesmith should have a record. There were only twenty-five made, and they cost a cool grand a piece. Pricey for a guy who drove a beater car."

"Okay," Ben said, stretching out the syllables. "I'm intrigued. Anything else?"

Jenny grinned. "Yep. He rented a place with a full kitchen, but it didn't look like he did much cooking. I saw a lot of take-out containers in the fridge and bags in the trash. But…he was an absolute fiend for Needhams and this weird brand of potato chips I'd never heard of. I looked them both up—only sold in Maine."

"What the hell is a Needham?"

Jenny looked smug. "It's a chocolate, potato, and coconut candy that's apparently a big deal up there."

"Potato?"

She shrugged and spread her hands in a "don't ask me" gesture. "I guess you've got to grow up with it. But from what I could see, he packed in a big supply of his favorite junk food for the trip. I didn't see any sales receipts, but I found a bag from Samson's Market. It's a family-owned grocery store chain that only has four stores—all of them in Maine. Here's the important part—Samson's caters to the coastal islands."

Ben blinked, putting the pieces together, and Jenny rushed ahead, clearly proud of her sleuthing.

"Don't you see? If Raines was in hiding, the islands in Maine would be perfect," Jenny went on enthusiastically. "They're remote, and they don't get much traffic or tourism. You could go up there and keep to yourself, and no one would bother you. But—" She looked triumphant. "Maine folks are known for being kinda clannish. They know if you're not 'from around' there. So they might have left him alone, but I bet you a bag of chips someone remembers him."

"That's brilliant," Ben said. "Now we just need a photo of him." He was certain that the manner of death hadn't left an identifiable face.

"I made a photocopy of his driver's license when he checked in," Jenny said. "You already found out that the address was phony, and the photo isn't great, but it might be good enough for someone to recognize him if he was a regular buying groceries."

"Great work." Ben's thoughts spun trying to figure out how to tie the pieces together. "Anything else?"

Jenny shook her head. "He traveled light. Rather sad. Either he didn't have much, or he didn't plan to stay very long."

"His car plates were New Jersey, registered to a different dead guy but not reported stolen," Ben told her. "The car's VIN was scratched off. Raines knew how to go deep undercover."

"But why come back?" Jenny leaned against the side of the doorway. "He had a sweet setup that lasted for twenty years and enough money that he could survive all that time. The bad people either couldn't find him or figured he was far enough away to not be a danger. He'd gotten away with whatever he did. So what was so important that he risked everything to come here?"

"That's a great question," Ben said. "And good sleuthing—you have just earned your pay for the week."

"And a bonus?" Jenny flashed a cheeky grin.

"I think that can be arranged."

Ben hurried back to his computer, eager to follow up on the leads Jenny had provided. He searched the addresses for Samson's Groceries and found the managers' names and contact information.

Just as he finished drafting an email requesting information about the man in the grainy photo, his phone rang.

"Hey, Ben? It's Monty," Montana Clark, the lighthouse keeper, said. "You got a minute?"

"Sure. What's up?"

"There's a ghost at the convent who wants to talk to someone about a murder."

Ben had a limited ability to see and hear ghosts, and he wasn't a full medium. Monty Clark, on the other hand, could summon spirits, make them visible to others, and even channel them in a séance. He was one of the most talented mediums Ben had ever met.

"Any particular murder?"

"Somebody named Tom Raines."

"I'll meet you at the lighthouse in twenty minutes." Ben reached for his wallet and keys.

"Something come up?" Jenny asked as he hurried past her desk.

"Going over to see Monty at the lighthouse. Might be another lead. I probably won't be back, so please close up."

"You got it, boss. See you tomorrow. Happy hunting, and don't let the ghosties bite."

Ben's thoughts tumbled as he drove. Erik's episode of PTSD the previous night shook Ben more than he wanted his partner to know. It broke his heart to see Erik so vulnerable and stripped of his defenses. Ben knew how strong and brave Erik really was and admired him for making such a successful new start. Glimpsing the fragility that went with that strength unsettled him.

I guess we all want to believe everyone else is unshakable because we know how shaky we are ourselves.

Most days, Ben could leave his past behind him. Years had passed since the worst times, and the move to Cape May had been healing in every way—especially his relationship with Erik. But on the darkest nights, Ben's mind forced him to confront how deep the damage went and recognize that the memories he tried so hard to bury were never far from the surface.

This morning, Erik had done his best to appear unfazed. They had talked about the incident, but Ben wasn't fooled into thinking that Erik had completely regained his balance.

There's a fine line between "fake it til you make it" and repression. Most days, Ben couldn't tell for certain which side of that line he was on.

Despite his worries about the recent move-in with Erik, Ben was glad he'd been there when the nightmares came. He hated to think how often Erik might have struggled through other times alone.

We're stronger together. And we can take better care of each other now.

Ben didn't doubt that moving in together was the right thing to do. He was more comfortable in his relationship with Erik, despite its newness, than he'd ever felt with any other boyfriend. None of his hesitation had to do with Erik; all of his doubts lay in his own suitability as a partner.

No one gets to be in their thirties without scratches and dents. We both might have a few more than most people, but we're familiar with the damage. Maybe that makes us better able to take care of each other.

The unwanted Raines case made Ben nervous. Somehow he and Erik had gotten personally tangled up in the situation despite their efforts to leave their old lives behind. They didn't know who had mailed the poker chips to Erik or why, but a possible connection to the Mob and the cursed hotel couldn't be good. Ben had no idea whether Raines had chosen his rental because of Ben's old police work, and if he had, why the link would matter.

In Ben's experience, loose ends were pitfalls. That meant he needed to get to the bottom of the situation fast.

Gravel crunched under his tires as he parked at the lighthouse. The Cape May Lighthouse jutted toward the sky, a white cylinder with a red cap. At the bottom, a small attached building held the gift shop and museum. Not far away was the keeper's cottage, where Monty lived.

This close to the shore, the brisk wind cut like a knife, cold and salty. Ben hesitated, not sure whether Monty was at the cottage or the gift shop.

"I'm over here." Monty opened the cottage door and gestured for Ben to come in.

The cozy dwelling went with Monty's job as a park ranger. Despite being more than a century old, renovations made it comfortable without losing the charm.

"Want some coffee?" Monty offered.

"I'd love some." Ben sat in one of the kitchen chairs as Monty poured for both of them and then settled across the table.

"Thanks for coming. Sister Frankie's expecting us, but I thought you might like a little background before we walk over to the convent."

Ben sipped his coffee, enjoying the hint of gingerbread flavoring. "St. Expeditus by the Sea, right?" The old Victorian complex had been a hotel before being purchased by a little-known group of consecrated monster hunters, Episcopalian priests and nuns who put their knowledge of the occult to work in the real world solving supernatural problems.

Monty nodded. "It's never actually been a convent, although that's the cover. It's more like a halfway house for ghosts who aren't sure whether they're ready to cross over. The spirits have unfinished business, and the staff help them find peace before they move on."

"What's Jon think of all that?"

Monty chuckled. "Jon and Sister Frankie have an agreement. He shepherds lost souls to the convent, and she doesn't try to recruit him."

Right on cue, a spoon skidded across the counter and into the sink, touched by invisible hands.

"Very dramatic, Jon," Monty said with a fond smile.

Ben could make out Jon's faint form, which grew nearly solid as Monty lent the ghost some of his energy. Jon Richards had been a movie stuntman before he had been murdered nearly seventy years ago on the beach near the lighthouse.

He knew a little of the ghost's story from what Monty had told him. Jon hadn't wanted to leave until he brought his killers to justice, and while he bided his time, he had been able to save several lives on the beach. When Jon met Monty, sparks flew, and the two of them fell in love—a real, if unconventional, partnership.

"I won't pretend to understand the convent's work, but I take it that she's got a ghost with a guilty conscience?"

Monty nodded, taking a gulp of his drink despite how hot it was. "Sometimes ghosts need to unburden themselves of the secrets they couldn't let go of in life. That can be difficult, especially if keeping the secret had been a really big deal. You'd think that being dead would change how people think about those things, but it's less of a difference than most people would believe."

"Anything I need to know before we go?" Ben finished his coffee and set the cup aside.

"Sister Frankie and I can help if the ghost needs extra energy to be seen and heard. I know you've got abilities, but I don't know how strong the ghost is. If they've got a long story to tell, some extra 'umph' can make the process easier."

"That will definitely help."

Monty took his last swallow and then carried both their cups to the sink. The water turned on to rinse them without Monty touching the faucet.

"Now you're just showing off," he teased Jon.

"The only other thing I'd tell you is that, no matter what the ghost tells us, don't react badly," Monty warned. "That could set the ghost back on its journey. Try to stay unemotional, even if the information is upsetting."

"Do you know what the ghost is going to say?"

Monty shook his head. "No. But it can't be anything good involving a murder."

Ben stood. "Let's see what's important enough for a message from beyond the grave."

Despite the short distance to the convent, Ben's teeth were chattering from the cold wind by the time they reached the sprawling compound of white clapboard buildings. As they entered the gates, Ben felt a frisson of energy from the presence of dozens of spirits. Nothing about the vibe felt dangerous or malicious, but even at a distance, he sensed their unrest.

Monty opened the door into the large foyer, and they stepped inside.

"I'm glad you're here." Sister Frankie hurried to greet them. "Good to see you both. Please, come with me."

Sister Frankie was a tall, lanky woman who might have been any age between late thirties and early fifties. Her sandy blond hair, shaved on one side, fell chin-length on the other. She wore a sweater over jeans, and the edges of a colorful tattoo peeked from beneath her sleeve.

The convent was simply furnished but not austere. Instead of the overdone Victorian furnishings that Ben expected based on the outside of the building, the pieces were more Shaker-inspired with clean, simple lines. Naturalist watercolors and botanical drawings provided restful accents.

They followed her into a small parlor with two wing chairs and a sofa. Sister Frankie took a seat in one of the chairs and motioned Ben and Monty to the couch.

"Sophia? Are you here? I've brought the guests you requested," Frankie called out to the empty room.

Ben felt the energy shift as a gray haze formed in the center of the parlor. He glanced at Monty, and the medium's eyes were closed, with an expression on his face of intense concentration. He wondered how the experience differed for Monty.

"I'll help her be seen and heard," Monty said quietly. "That way you can focus on what she has to tell us."

The ghost took shape, an older woman who looked to be in her seventies with short pale hair and a slender build. "I'm Sophia Calasso," she said, looking shy but determined. "I was once in love with Tom Raines, long ago. He disappeared, and I lost track of him until his soul passed on just a few days ago."

"Why did you stay, Sophia?" Sister Frankie asked in a gentle tone.

"I had a good life after Tom left. I married and had a family, a career. Lived a long time," the ghost replied. "But I'm afraid to move on because I knew things went on that were wrong, and I don't know what that means for my soul."

"Someone else's actions are not your fault," Sister Frankie replied.

"I kept his secret," Sophia said. "I knew he did bad things, and I didn't do anything to stop him."

"Tom worked for the Mafia," Ben said. "You wouldn't have stopped what was going on, and you might have gotten yourself killed."

"I was afraid," Sophia confessed. "Not of Tom—I saw a different side of him. He didn't talk much about his work, but I knew he was an accountant for shady people. It wore on him. He was scared of them."

"It's healthy to be scared of those people," Ben assured her. "They're bad news."

"Tom was bitter when he drank," Sophia said in a reluctant tone. "He held a grudge against his grandfather. Said that his granddad 'held out on him' and ruined his life."

He probably knew that his granddad hid a large haul and didn't share it with him. Especially if his father was killed over a treasure he never benefitted from.

"Did he ever say more?" Sister Frankie asked.

"About what his grandfather did? No. I knew better than to ask. But it was strange—just before Tom disappeared, his mood changed. He seemed happier, not as angry at the world. Said something about 'making up for the inheritance that was stolen from him.' I didn't think that made any sense, but he didn't explain. And then he was gone."

"Did you hear from him at all after he left town?" Ben's intuition told him that the ghost was telling the truth, at least as much of it as she knew.

"No. I had no idea he intended to leave. I hoped that we would get married," Sophia said. "He quit his job, and people came asking about him, but I couldn't tell them anything. Some of them were mad, and I was scared of them, but they finally left me alone."

"How did you know he died?" Ben couldn't help feeling curious.

"I sensed his spirit." The ghost sounded embarrassed. "I guess I always carried a torch for him despite everything. He didn't contact me. But I knew he was gone."

"Is that why you chose to talk about the past now?" Sister Frankie looked intrigued.

"Yes. I'm tired and ready to move forward," Sophia said. "I just didn't want to end up in a bad place because of what I knew."

"Please set your fear aside," Sister Frankie said. "You could not have stopped the situation, and you would have put yourself in danger. I'm sure it didn't feel like it at the time, but Tom did you a favor removing you from his life. You would never have been safe."

"If I move on...will I end up *down there?*" The ghost's voice trembled.

"You did not commit a crime. Knowing about something you can't change is not a sin," Sister Frankie reassured. "Would you like to cross over now?"

Sophia nodded. "Yes, please. Thank you for hearing my confession."

Sister Frankie spoke words of absolution and blessing. Sophia's image dimmed until she finally vanished.

Monty let out a sigh and relaxed against the back of his seat. Ben guessed it had taken a lot of energy for him to help the ghost to be seen.

"More proof that Raines's grandfather really did pull off a big score," Ben observed. "And if Tom suddenly perked up before he disappeared, that squares with him embezzling a fortune for himself —making up for the money he didn't get from his dad."

"Or maybe he figured out how to rip off the people he worked for to set himself up in comfort while he kept looking for granddaddy's loot," Monty countered. "But why did he come back to Cape May, and did someone kill him because of his grandfather's missing money?"

"Plus, we still don't know who sent the poker chips to Erik and what they mean," Ben added. "Raines's killer is out there. I want to get to the bottom of this in case, for some reason, he comes after Erik and me."

"I wasn't sure what Sophia's ghost would tell you," Sister Frankie said. "Was it helpful?"

Ben nodded. "We know more than we did before. I'm still missing a couple of pieces of the puzzle. Thank you."

Sister Frankie smiled. "Any time. It's not uncommon for ghosts to want to clear the air before they move on, and even though they're dead, it can take a surprising amount of time for them to work up the courage, especially when they feel guilty. Thank you for hearing her out—I think that helped her be at peace."

She walked them back to the door. "How's that man of yours?" she teased Monty.

Monty grinned. "Treating me very well," he assured her. "He says 'hello'—from a safe distance."

"He makes it sound like this is some sort of hellmouth that sucks in souls." Sister Frankie chuckled. "We're really more of a transfer station or a base camp. Odd as it may be."

They said goodbye, and Monty promised to stay in touch. Outside, Ben swore the wind had grown even colder.

"What did you make of that?" he asked Monty. "I'm never sure whether other people with abilities see the same things I do."

"There might be a slight variation of how detailed ghost's appearance seems from one medium to another, but I don't think I got any insider information," Monty replied. "I suspect that Sophia told us a mostly true story."

"Mostly?" Ben glanced over to his companion, intrigued.

"People tend to put themselves in a good light even when they're confessing their 'sins,'" Monty replied. "I think all of what she told us was true—but not the whole truth. I got the feeling that back in the day, she would have still gone along with Tom's role in the 'family business' if he had stuck around and been happy to spend the old man's money if Tom could have found it."

Ben thought for a moment, then nodded. "She wasn't feeling guilt over things being illegal. She was worried that *not* minding would get her in trouble in the afterlife."

Monty nodded. "Yes, that's what I got out of it."

"Still, it's an interesting perspective. I wonder if the person who sent Erik the poker chips had the same sort of internal struggle," Ben mused. "They knew about the heist on some level and kept the secret, passing down the chips, but knowing that it was wrong and that they might be putting their heirs in danger."

"Sounds like a reasonable theory to me," Monty said as they left the beach and headed across the parking lot toward the lighthouse. "Would you like to come in and warm up?"

Ben shook his head. "Thanks, but I need to get home. Tell Jon I said goodbye."

He glanced at his watch and figured Erik was still at the shop, so he called Sean.

"You doing anything?" he asked when Sean picked up.

"Depends. What are you offering?"

"I want to see if Tom Raines's ghost has shown up yet," Ben replied. "I didn't pick up anything the day of the murder, but sometimes it takes ghosts a little while to get their shit together."

"Can't imagine why," Sean said in a droll tone. "I met up with some friends, but I was just heading back. I can meet you at the office."

"See you in a few." Ben ended the call. He went back over the conversation with the ghost at the convent as he drove and wondered how many other women who had married into the Mob had shared the same misgivings.

He'd seen enough ripped-from-the-headlines Mafia movies and true crime documentaries to have heard tearful women swear they really thought their husbands were legitimately in the waste management business. While he didn't doubt that most of the wives and mistresses had been kept out of the main business dealings for their own protection—as well as because of the Mob's well-known misogyny—he had never believed that they didn't suspect.

I think they knew on some level, even if they didn't let themselves admit it fully. People can be willfully ignorant in amazing ways if their standard of living is on the line.

As far as Ben had been able to find out, Tom Raines never married. That made sense since he had gone into self-imposed exile. He wouldn't dare tell a spouse the full truth out of fear of betrayal and for their own safety. The lies would eventually erode the relationship.

Three generations of ruined lives, all for greed. No payoff is worth that.

He parked the car and found Sean in the break room with a cup of coffee. "I need to grab a few things," he told his cousin and went to get a bag he kept under his desk. He and Erik ran into hauntings often enough that Ben had put a kit together to mobilize faster. The small duffel contained plenty of salt, bottles of iron filings, a couple of crowbars, and chalk for drawing sigils.

"Old Tom might not show," Ben said as they drove to the unit. "Either because he can't muster the mojo, or he just doesn't want to."

"Never thought ghosts would have a problem getting it up," Sean snarked.

"Somehow, I knew you were going to go there." Ben gave an exaggerated sigh.

"Hey—gotta stay 'on brand,'" Sean teased. "People have expectations."

"Next thing, you'll be talking about yourself in the third person," Ben groaned.

"We'll let that one slide."

Ben fished a wrapped hard candy out of his pocket and threw it at Sean, bouncing it off his shoulder.

"Ow! I should call a cop. That's assault."

"We've both done worse wrestling for the remote. And you'd only call the cops because you think Hendricks is cute." Ben gave him the side-eye.

"It's not my fault that men in uniform are hot," Sean protested.

"He's straight as far as I know."

"*As far as you know,* leaves a lot of room," Sean pointed out, arching an eyebrow.

"You've been watching too much role-play sexy cop porn again, haven't you? Don't answer that."

Sean gave an evil chuckle in reply.

"Hey—look at the car." Ben parked, and they walked to Tom's old junker. "Someone jimmied the locks." The trunk lid was ajar, and one of the doors had scratches near the handle.

"Do you think they found anything?" Sean walked in a slow circle around the vehicle.

Ben shook his head. "Doubt it. Tom didn't hide from the Mob for thirty years by being careless. And I think he came to Cape May to find something he didn't have, not because of something he already owned. Besides, the cops already searched the place."

"Maybe you can get the ghost to tell you."

"That's exactly what I'm hoping to do." Ben paused at the door to the unit Tom rented, stretching out his senses. He didn't pick up on ghostly energy, but he knew that sometimes spirits could retreat out of range and still be aware of what was going on.

He and Sean stepped into the apartment. Despite the efforts of the crime scene cleaners, it still didn't smell right. The scent of blood was gone, but the overly sanitized odor of cleaning products and air fresheners was a giveaway that something worse had been laundered away.

Ben hurried to put down a salt circle around them and reinforced it with a heavier salt-soaked blessed rope. "Hold this." He handed Sean a crowbar. "If an angry ghost shows up, whack him with it."

"I thought we wanted the ghost to show?"

"We do—if he's reasonably friendly."

Ben finished the protective circle and stood, picking up a second crowbar. "Thomas Raines. Show yourself. We've got questions. And for what it cost to clean up your mess, you owe me."

The room stayed eerily quiet. Then the temperature plunged to freezing, and a gust of wind nearly ripped the curtains from their rods, lashing them like sails in a storm. It carried away some of the loose salt, but the cord held.

The wind swirled like a vortex, sweeping the check-out time tent card and take-out menus off the chest of drawers and rattling the lampshades.

"Do you know who killed you?" Ben yelled above the racket. When no answer came, he tried again. "Did you find your grandfather's loot? Is that why you came back?"

The wind grew dark like smoke, and a face formed in the billowing clouds. "It's mine. You can't have it!"

"Can't spend money in hell," Ben observed. "But we can keep your killer from getting away with stealing your stash if you tell us who did it."

"Leave that to me!" The ghost pressed his smoke face against the energy boundary of the salt circle until the features distorted monstrously.

"He can't reach us as long as the barrier holds," Ben warned Sean, who looked wild-eyed.

"Mind your mouth. We have a friend of a friend who's a necromancer," Ben told the ghost. "He can send your foggy ass off to the afterlife with a snap of his fingers, and then you won't get your money or your revenge."

"Get out!"

"This is my fucking rental that you're haunting!" Ben shouted back. "Either help us solve your murder or go to hell, but get out of my unit!"

The wind screamed in the confines of the room, battering all but the largest furniture. Then as abruptly as it started, the fury ended, leaving Ben and Sean gripping their crowbars white-knuckled and hunched defensively against another attack.

"Do you think he's gone?" Sean kept his voice low, as if the ghost might hear.

Ben listened with his ability. "He's not here right now. No guarantee he won't come back."

"Do you really know an exorcist?"

"A necromancer *and* an exorcist," Ben replied with a chuckle. "Friends of friends. But Erik and Alessia can handle Tom. They took care of a bigger, badder ghost at the Regent Theater."

Sean shuddered. "I had finally mostly forgotten about that, thanks."

"If Tom is a problem or if we need to get more out of him, I can have Monty give it a try." Ben gathered the salted rope and locked the apartment. "He just handled a ghost at the convent, and I didn't want to stretch him too thin. He's an actual medium—I'm just a guy who can talk to ghosts."

"Would it make a difference?"

Ben shrugged as he and Sean walked back to the office. "I don't know. Monty certainly isn't going to channel Tom's ghost, and ethically, he can't compel Tom to do anything. I think for now, Tom's given us all he's going to. He might change his mind later."

"Is that a good thing or a bad thing?"

Ben sighed. "I guess that depends on what he might have to say."

SIX

ERIK

"I s it just me?" Susan asked after she had wrapped up a customer's purchase and sent them on their way. "Or do you feel jittery too?"

Erik smiled. "I feel it. The autumn equinox is a couple of days away—and that juices up the genius loci at the old Commodore Wilson hotel site."

"You mean I've been feeling like this because of a damn hotel that isn't even there anymore?"

Erik moved around the store, straightening items that had been handled by customers and tidying displays. "Not the hotel itself—the land beneath it. Or rather, the inherent energy in that piece of ground. To put it another way—bad mojo."

"I've lived here all my life. How come I never heard about that before?"

Erik reshelved a book that had been left on a table and carried a pair of opera glasses back to the place they belonged. "Alessia and her coven have been doing containment rituals for years. Probably other witches before them. Plus, you didn't work at Trinkets before, even if you were friendly with Mr. Pettis. This shop soaks up energy like a sponge, and the equinox is going to change the resonance."

"Once the equinox is over, will the energy go back down?" Susan polished a set of silver candlesticks at the counter as she spoke.

"It doesn't ever go away completely, but it should drop to a dull hum until the winter solstice," Erik replied.

"I'm surprised more people don't notice." She worked on a stubborn spot of tarnish.

"They do—they just don't know what to call it." Erik leaned into the window to adjust a vase that had shifted. "They blame the weather or say they're having an off day. Why would they think anything else? The genius loci is a permanent fixture of the land. Since it's always been here, people take the vibration as something normal, like the tides."

"I feel antsy." Susan finished the candlestick and picked up a silver picture frame to polish. "But what's it like for you, with your abilities?"

Erik paused trying to figure out how to put the feeling into words. "In the shop, I'm hyper-aware of pieces that carry psychic residue. Like there's a steady buzz just at the edge of what I can hear. We only have pieces with good energy on display, so it's not unpleasant. The stuff in the safe, on the other hand—"

He shivered. "That gets amped up too. Which is why I'm glad it's a lead-lined, iron box."

"Are you any closer to figuring out the deal with the poker chips?" Susan asked.

"Beyond confirming that they were from the Fun Factory and finding out a little more about the place—no. I've got a sneaking suspicion there will turn out to be a connection to the dead guy at Ben's rental unit, and the bad energy from the old hotel site will make everything worse."

Erik brushed away some dust on one of the mahogany display cases. The old store had good bones, with a big window facing the street and antique cabinets and bookshelves that showed off the merchandise in style.

While the tea sets, vintage paintings, small furnishings, and decorative items were far different from the Old Master artwork he dealt with in his previous job, Erik appreciated the calm energy of these pieces. Because they had been used by regular people in their everyday lives, the items in the store felt grounded and satisfied. Museum artwork, on the other hand, often had a cold, distant resonance, perhaps because they were exhibited in a public space with no human contact.

The genius loci's hum felt like the faint buzz of electrical wires, just at the edge of perception but still a constant annoyance. Between peaks, the resonance dulled to be nearly imperceptible. Erik wondered how anyone had been able to spend time in the Commodore Wilson without feeling the energy and suspected that whether or not people knew what made them uncomfortable, that probably contributed to the hotel's downfall.

"Did you hear about the break-in?"

Susan's question jolted Erik from his thoughts.

"Robbery?"

"Not sure. I have a police monitor, although Cole wishes I didn't," she confessed. "The call went out last night. Someone broke into a house and ransacked it. The owner was an elderly woman who either fell or was hit by the burglar. She went to the hospital."

Erik walked back up toward the counter. "Could they tell if anything was taken?"

Susan shook her head. "Not that anyone said over the radio. I feel bad for that poor woman. Hope they catch the bastard soon."

"Yeah, that's a terrible thing," Erik agreed. A hunch told him to pay attention. Cape May had a low crime rate, especially compared to cities Erik was used to, like Atlanta or London. Usually, problems spiked during tourist season with car break-ins, unattended items on the beach, or the occasional pickpocket. In the off-season, when the population was mostly locals, car wrecks, DUIs, and domestic disputes were more likely to fill the police blotter.

Not counting the time or two Ben and Erik unintentionally ignited a Mob war.

"Do you know anything about the victim? Has there been a rash of break-ins? There's probably no connection to the murder at the hotel and the poker chips, but I've learned the hard way that nothing is really a coincidence," Erik said, explaining when Susan gave him a puzzled look.

She pulled up a site on her phone. "Robberies usually go down in the off-season with fewer people coming through town. Violent break-ins are pretty rare here." Susan scanned the article.

"According to the local news, her name is Dolores Quinn, and she is sixty-eight. Neighbors called the police because they heard shouting. The attacker went out the back door and got away."

Erik frowned. "They haven't caught whoever killed the guy in the rental unit. The two attacks might not be connected, but—"

"Cape May doesn't have a murder problem—most of the time." Susan arched her eyebrow.

Erik knew she was teasing him, but he still felt a pang of responsibility. He and Ben seemed to find the skeletons in all the closets, sometimes literally. Fortunately, they hadn't been run out of town yet.

"She's sixty-eight. Raines, the guy in the rental unit, was in his seventies. Did they know each other? Was there a connection somewhere?"

"I didn't know Dolores—she's older than me, so we wouldn't have been in school together, but the family name sounds familiar." Susan offered a chagrined smile. "Cape May isn't a big place, but we aren't all acquainted, no matter what the tourists think. Especially if someone isn't in a job with a lot of public contact, like at a store or a restaurant. Let me see what I can dig up."

Erik went in the back and called Ben. "Everything okay?"

"Why wouldn't it be?" Ben sounded puzzled. "I've got some things to fill you in on, but nothing bad. What's up?"

"There was a break-in," Erik told him. "It might be nothing—but an older woman's house was ransacked. It sounds like someone might be looking for something."

"The poker chips?"

"It's a stretch. Doesn't make sense that it would be. And yet I can't get that possibility out of my mind. In fact, that's the only thing on my radar, those poker chips," Erik said. "Of course, it might be completely unrelated."

"Because our lives always work like that," Ben said in a dry tone.

"Right." Erik hesitated. "We don't know what game is being played, but if this is all connected to that long-ago heist. People will do awful things to get their hands on a fortune. Just be careful."

"Yeah, you too. I'm working a couple of angles—I'll fill you in at dinner. Love you."

"Love you." Erik ended the call and leaned against the break room counter, staring at the darkened screen as his thoughts whirled.

There's a logic to all this. We just don't know how to look at it. If it's related, then this makes sense to someone, and we'd better catch on soon.

"I've got something," Susan called out from the shop, and Erik hurried to the counter.

"I found the obituary for Dolores's mother," Susan explained. "Apparently, they owned Quinn Private Home Services, which provided contract housekeeping. The obit says the company was started by the grandmother, Eleanor, and that both Dolores and her mother, Opal, also worked there."

"Interesting. Anything else?"

"Dolores herself seems to have stayed out of the spotlight," Susan said. "But in the mother's obituary, it doesn't mention Dolores having a spouse or children. When I looked up Quinn Private Home Services, I found a listing on a local business website with a note that the company was closed."

"Huh," Erik said, feeling like an important connection was dangling beyond his grasp. "Were they cleaners or true house-keepers?"

"What do you mean?"

"Cleaning services come in and tidy up. But when I lived in Atlanta, a lot of workaholics like me hired a private housekeeper who ran everything because we were too busy. They supervised cleaners and personal chefs and lawn services, ordered groceries, made sure the bills were paid, and handled picking up packages from the front office or babysitting repair workers," Erik said.

"It wasn't cheap, but for people who work long hours or travel a lot—or only are in seasonal residence—it's a godsend. Good money if you've got a knack for it."

"That describes a lot of people in Cape May," Susan replied. "I could see that going over with some of our wealthier residents."

"It wasn't just corporate types." Erik winced because he had certainly been very well-off in his former job. "In my apartment building in Atlanta, there were some retirees who hired services like that. I always figured in those cases that the housekeeper helped keep track of appointments, made sure they got to doctor visits, and tracked caregiver schedules. Things a son or daughter might do if people had a family."

"That would be a fantastic service," Susan agreed. "And if they charged for what they were worth, they wouldn't need many clients."

"Dammit," Erik muttered. "This opens up a whole new can of worms. Did Dolores work for someone connected to Raines? He was in Maine, so it wasn't him. She was retired, so there weren't current customers—a thief wouldn't be looking for passwords or house keys."

"Opal died ten years ago." Susan glanced at her phone. "The business closed five years later, so Dolores has been retired for a while. In that time, I imagine some of her clients passed on as well. Anyone who was that involved in the workings of a household might know some unpleasant secrets about clients, but the longer time goes by, the less valuable those secrets become."

"It depends on the secret," Erik countered. "Dolores might not have known anything, but maybe someone *thought* she did."

His phone rang, and Jaxon's name showed up. "Hi! What's up?"

"Maybe nothing," Jaxon said. "But you're the one who doesn't believe in coincidence, so I'm letting you know about something odd. An old acquaintance from my Broadway days just showed up in town, Holden Carr. We were in a few shows together and palled around at the time, kept in touch online, but I haven't seen him in years.

"Turns out he's the nephew of the guy who died in Ben's rental unit," Jaxon went on. "The only next-of-kin. He came to collect the dead man's personal effects and claim the body."

"That's...odd," Erik agreed.

"Right? He stopped in at the Center to chat me up about the town. I told him a lot without telling him anything if you know what I mean. After he left, I got thinking about back in New York City, and how when Holden got drunk—and we all drank a lot back then—he would go on about how some of his family was Mobbed up and that his great-grandfather supposedly pulled off a big heist, but no one ever found the money."

Erik's eyes widened. "Did he have details?"

"If he did, he never shared them. We all thought he was blowing smoke out of his ass at the time. Even other theater people thought he was dramatic."

"Do you think he's dangerous?" Erik's mind went into high gear coming up with ominous possibilities.

"Anyone's dangerous if the stakes are high enough. Holden tagged along sometimes with my group, but he wasn't really one of us. Acting on Broadway is a brutal business, but my inner circle wasn't cut-throat. Holden had that edge, like he'd throw someone under the bus to get what he wanted. I never trusted him," Jaxon said.

"Do you think he's here looking for the money?"

"Of course he is. He's an actor. We like expensive things." Jaxon paused. "There was always a darkness to Holden. He was fascinated with the occult and ran with some goths who took things too far. The guy looks like an Ivy League fair-haired nepo baby, but he gravitated toward creepy roles. And when he got drunk, he used to say that he 'made a deal with the devil' for his success."

"None of that sounds good," Erik said.

"I didn't want him dropping my name and having you think I vouched for him. Watch your back—and warn Ben."

"I will. Thanks for the heads-up."

"Cape May was boring before you and Ben showed up," Jaxon replied with a laugh. "Gotta keep you both safe."

Erik tried to call Ben, but he didn't pick up. "Shit."

"Something wrong?" Susan stepped halfway into the back room while keeping an eye on a shopper browsing in the store.

"Jaxon just warned me about a suspicious person, and I can't get Ben on the phone to pass it on."

Susan jerked her head toward the door. "Go over to his office. I'll hold the fort."

"You're awesome." Erik grabbed his coat and headed outside. Half a block away, he paused to do a search on Jaxon's acquaintance and came up with plenty of promo photos.

Holden Carr looked to be in his early forties, handsome in a Country Club sort of way. Erik could imagine him portraying college boys in his younger days and their wealthy fathers now. A quick glance at Carr's professional bio showed that he worked steadily, but despite his drunken confession hadn't had a breakout role.

At least I'll recognize him if I bump into him, Erik thought, pocketing his phone and promising to look into Carr's background more closely later.

Tom Raines embezzled a pile of cash and got away with it for a long time. Maybe he didn't spend it all, and there's a nest egg left. His grandfather ripped off the Mob and hid the money so well no one ever found it. Which stash is Carr looking for?

Erik resisted the temptation to jog the rest of the way. When he got to Nolan Resort Real Estate, a late-model, midnight blue BMW sat at the curb. Erik admired the pricy sports car and bet it was a rental.

Carr's here. Trying to make an impression.

Erik weighed his options. If Ben was already talking with Carr, Erik was too late to pass along a warning. Then again, Ben's years as a cop meant he was street-savvy enough not to let anything important slip, and Carr didn't have a reason to get violent.

He decided to bide his time and slipped into the coffee shop across the street where he had a good view of the real estate office front door.

"The usual?" Katie, the barista asked when Erik walked in. He and Ben were regulars.

"Make it two, please." Erik kept his attention on the office.

"Did you and Ben get a sexy new car?" she asked as she pulled the shots.

Erik laughed. "Nah. Not our style, although it's pretty. Must be some New York hotshot on vacation."

"Yeah, we get plenty of those, although not so much in the off-season," she agreed. "Ben's a good-looking guy. When are you gonna lock that up by putting a ring on it?"

"We just moved in together," Erik joked. "I'm working up to it."

Steam hissed as she made the lattes. "Just looking out for you two. You gotta move fast when the right one comes along."

Erik paid for the drinks and took a seat by the window, biding his time. Fifteen minutes later, a man who resembled Carr's photo emerged, dressed in a sport coat and dress slacks. He hustled down the steps, got into the car and drove away. Erik thought he looked tense, and not completely pleased.

"Hey, got time for coffee?" Erik asked Ben when his call went through. "I'm across the street."

Minutes later, Ben joined him. "You must have ESP. This is exactly what I needed." Ben took a sip of his drink.

"I can't blame this one on a vision—it's Jaxon's fault." Erik filled Ben in on his conversation.

"Were you here in time to see Carr? What did you think?"

Erik nodded. "I thought he fit Jaxon's description to a 'T.' How about you?"

Ben sat back, cradling his take-out cup in both hands. "Carr wanted to make an impression that he was important. The way people who aren't usually act."

Erik chuckled, knowing what Ben meant. "What else?"

"I'll confirm this with Cole, but Carr made it sound like he heard about Raines from the cops. Although as a nephew it's odd that he'd be on paperwork—especially since Raines vanished for twenty years. Carr had to have been fairly young when Raines went missing."

"I wondered about that. Maybe they tracked Raines to a sister who's deceased, and found the son."

"Maybe, but I think it's sketchy." Ben paused for another sip. The blissful expression and happy murmur he made sent a rush of heat to Erik's groin.

"Keep your mind out of the gutter," Ben teased. "We're in public."

"You just seemed to need some alone time with your latte," Erik joked back.

"I'll take you up on 'alone time' later," Ben promised.

"So what happened when Carr showed up?" The more Erik thought about the whole situation, the fishier it seemed.

"He showed up looking and acting like an entitled jackass and said he was there to claim his dead uncle's property," Ben replied. "I asked him for ID, tried to figure out how he knew about Raines's death, and did my best to stall while Jenny checked out his license and address. That part, at least, was legit."

"And?"

Ben shrugged. "I told him that I couldn't just hand things over without talking first with the police. They released the apartment as a crime scene and let us box up Raines's things, but they still have whatever they took when they were here. Plus I want to make real sure they're actually done with everything before I let some New York douchebag just walk off with everything."

They finished their coffees and headed back to work, promising each other to be extra careful.

Erik stayed alert as he walked to Trinkets, wondering what Carr's next move would be. Since Raines's self-imposed exile made it impossible for him to have been close to his uncle, it amazed Erik that Carr even knew much about Raines, although perhaps his notoriety had made him a family legend.

He's either after whatever remains of Raines's money—or he thinks Raines came back here looking for Edwin's hidden treasure.

Unless Tom Raines had established some legitimate employment during his time in Maine—which would have been difficult without a solid false identity—any money that remained would probably be seized as being part of his embezzlement loot.

Of course, Carr might figure that Raines hid his stash outside of banks and legal channels, and have daydreams of gold bars stacked in a hidden safe in the wilds of Maine.

That might be possible, although Erik couldn't imagine trucking heavy and difficult to exchange gold onto an island in Maine without piquing the notice of even the most standoffish and indifferent neighbors.

Did Carr kill Raines? Sure, he told Jaxon he just came to Cape May today, but who's to say? Maybe he managed to find his missing uncle and tracked him here earlier. After all, Raines hadn't left Maine for decades, so for him to suddenly risk a road trip had to be important.

But Raines was shot execution-style. Carr was an actor, not a hitman. Did he kill Raines like that to throw everyone off the track? Or is there a Mob killer loose in town—and did he get what he wanted from Raines, or is he still looking for his payoff?

To keep his thoughts from spiraling, Erik threw himself into doing inventory when he got back to the shop. Susan seemed to recognize his mood and gave him space while still checking in from time to time. He figured the box of fresh donuts in the break room was a gesture of concern and wolfed down two of the chocolate-iced glazed sweets with a hot cup of coffee.

I wish we could ask Chief Hendricks about Dolores Quinn's attack. But we've got no need to know, and so far, no connection beyond intuition. Without anything stronger, I hate to ask one of our hacker friends to break into the system. We need to keep Hendricks on our side.

I like living here. I don't want the chief of police as an enemy.

After a couple of hours of dedicated inventory-taking, Susan laid a hand on his arm. "Are you okay? You seem...preoccupied."

Erik appreciated Susan's concern, so different from his own stand-offish mother. "I am. Sorry for being bad company today. I'm worried about the weird things going on and hoping they don't end up pulling Ben and me into more trouble."

"Don't borrow trouble," she told him. "I'm sure Cole would have called if he thought either of you were in danger."

Erik didn't doubt that the chief would protect them if things came down to the wire. But he also knew that Hendricks took a dim view of Ben's private investigator efforts and his own informal sleuthing, even though visions and ghosts provided information not readily available through conventional methods.

"Maybe no news is good news," Erik agreed, although he didn't completely believe his own words.

Susan face-palmed herself. "Ugh—I totally forgot. Remember when I asked Steve at the archive to help us look into the Fun Factory? He called me back while you were with Ben. I swear he's an awesome detective in his own right."

"Historians usually are—and they've got to piece together clues long after the witnesses are dead," Erik replied.

"You knew that the Fun Factory burned and that it was owned by the same man who owned the Commodore Wilson, right?"

Erik nodded and felt his pulse speed up, hoping for a break.

"According to Steve, there were rumors that the night the fire broke out, the manager of the casino made off with all the money." Susan seemed to relish the details as if the hundred-year-old gossip was fresh tea.

"Did the manager set the fire? Or was it the Atlantic City Mob? Or did the owner have bigger money problems and torch the place himself?" Erik asked.

"According to Steve, the fire's origin was never fully explained. It might have been suspicious, but apparently there was never enough evidence to press charges, although the insurance company quibbled. They eventually paid out, but much less than the full value, which was said to contribute to the owner's bankruptcy with the Commodore Wilson."

"How does everything keep coming back to that damned place?" Erik muttered.

"But wait—there's more," Susan teased. "The name of the casino manager was Edwin Raines."

"Raines?" Erik echoed.

Susan nodded, looking pleased with herself. "Tom Raines's grandfather. Edwin was later murdered, but no one ever claimed to find the money. Rumor had it that three million went missing, which would be around ninety million in today's dollars."

"People have killed for a lot less," Erik said. He caught Susan up on Holden Carr. "If he was Tom Raines's nephew, then Edwin would be his great-grandfather. Jaxon said Carr used to get drunk and talk about a lost treasure. What if Carr was as obsessed with finding it as Tom was?"

"Steve also found out that Galen Raines, Edwin's son and Tom's father, was under suspicion of ties to Atlantic City and Newark mobsters. Bad decisions ran in the family," she remarked. "Galen was suspected of several thefts and was murdered as well."

"Quite a family history," Erik said. "The chief told Ben that there was a connection to one of his old cases in Newark—that had to be Galen or another relative. Edwin would have already died, and Tom was missing during those years."

"Steve said it didn't look like Galen was a big player," Susan said. "Of course, it takes an army of functionaries to run the Mob, not just hitmen and wise guys."

Erik still marveled at how matter-of-factly people in New Jersey talked about organized crime.

"Thank you—and thank Steve. We've got a connection now to the Fun Factory *and* the Commodore Wilson—and a solid link to the Raines family. I just don't know what that has to do with the poker chips and whether Holden Carr is a treasure hunter or a killer."

"Oh, an interesting piece of trivia. Steve is kind of an unofficial expert on the Jersey Mafia," Susan said. "What can I say? Some people are serial killer fans, and Steve knows about mobsters. You ever see that television series about the Atlantic City Mob back in the Prohibition days? They modeled the main guy after Nucky Johnson, who ran the Boardwalk syndicate back then. If he didn't like the Fun Factory muscling in on his territory, he might have taken action to make it go away."

"Good info," Erik said. "I'm just not sure how to put all the pieces together."

Erik polished off his coffee and set the cup aside reluctantly before heading out to the front to give Susan a break. During the off-season, Trinkets kept shorter hours, although unlike some stores and restaurants, they remained open, at least for this first year. Erik wanted to use the time to build up the blog and website.

He figured if he was going to be working online he might as well keep the store open for walk-ins, appointments, and going through new purchases from estate sales and auctions.

Erik was busy adding some vintage Christmas ornaments to the inventory when the bell over the door jangled. He looked up as Holden Carr strolled into the shop. Erik hoped he controlled his expression, feeling surprised and dismayed.

What is he doing here?

"Hi. Welcome to Trinkets. How may I help you?"

Carr flashed a high-wattage smile that must have been a hit in his Broadway days. "I just happened by and wanted to look around."

"Please do. Just ask if you have any questions." Erik hoped he sounded welcoming instead of uncomfortable.

Carr walked through the store, not touching anything. While he meandered up and down the aisles, he didn't linger. Even casual shoppers who loved antiques tended to get "stuck" when their eyes caught an object of interest. Erik had the feeling Carr was making a show of browsing.

"Were you looking for something in particular?" Erik asked from behind the counter.

"Do you carry any occult objects?" Carr asked off-handedly like he didn't really care, but his body language told Erik that the newcomer was paying close attention.

"You mean like Ouija boards?" Erik replied, deliberately misunderstanding.

Carr laughed and shook his head. "No—real stuff. Amulets. Chalices. Grimoires."

"Can't say we get much call for that sort of thing," Erik lied. Anything with real power either went to Alessia for safekeeping or, for malicious items, waited in the safe until Erik's contact from Charleston could come collect them to be neutralized. Locals knew to look for anything witchy at Alessia's store, in the back room.

"I would have thought strange things might turn up in a place like Cape May," Carr said, still giving the shelves a desultory glance. "After all, it's one of the most haunted towns on the coast."

"As you can see, we get a lot of timepieces, housewares, decorative items, and small furnishings." Erik tried to remain nonchalant. "We only handle larger pieces if they're truly unique. What we stock generally comes from estate sales in the greater Cape May area."

"Do you believe in ghosts?" Carr turned to glance over his shoulder at Erik, who couldn't decide whether he was being toyed with or interrogated.

"I think everyone's seen things they can't explain," Erik answered. "I try to be open minded."

With a sincere questioner, Erik would have been more straightforward, but he felt like he and Carr were playing a semantic game of cat and mouse.

"Didn't Cape May have a lot of film production here long ago?" Carr asked.

Erik nodded. "Back in the 1950s and early sixties there were a lot of movies made here. Mostly beach comedies, but some suspense flicks as well. They're pretty good if you can find them on disk. The old theater in town was just refurbished too."

Monty's ghostly partner, Jon Richards, had been a stunt actor in those movies before his murder, so Erik had heard a lot of stories about those years.

"You ever hear of a place called the Commodore Wilson?" Carr seemed to watch Erik for his reaction. "My great-grandfather worked for the guy who owned it at the time."

"I've heard of it, but it was gone long before I came here," Erik replied. "It must have been quite a showplace in its time." *In addition to being haunted, cursed, and built on top of a malicious nature spirit.*

"It's always sad when those old landmarks go away," Carr said. "You ever get any memorabilia from them?"

"Sometimes. That sort of thing gets snatched up by collectors as soon as it hits the shelf," Erik answered, which was mostly true. He wondered what Carr was fishing for.

He could be legitimately curious about the Commodore Wilson because of family ties. Could he possibly know about the Fun Factory? Almost no one remembers it. Two relatives of the Fun Factory's crooked manager show up in town, and one ends up dead. What's the connection? And do those poker chips have anything to do with it?

Given Jaxon's warning, Erik wasn't going to mention the chips, not until he had a better idea of the game being played.

"Are you from Cape May?"

Erik shook his head. "Not originally. Just moved here this year." He held his breath, hoping Susan didn't pick this moment to appear. His gut told him to share as little as possible with Carr.

"I had family here a long time ago, but I was raised outside Newark and spent quite a long while in New York City," Carr added. "Some of it on Broadway. I'm an actor."

"Sounds interesting," Erik said non-committedly. "What brings you to town?"

"My uncle died. I'm his only family, so I came to handle things."

Interesting. It's true...but not the whole truth. Is he hiding the rest, or just not over-sharing?

"I'm sorry for your loss."

Carr shrugged. "We weren't close. I hadn't seen him since I was a kid, but there was no one else—so here I am."

I'd buy his act—if Jaxon hadn't told me that he'd talked about the family rumor of his great-grandfather's big missing heist. Did he and Tom Raines just happen to come to Cape May at nearly the same time looking for the money? Or did they meet up—with deadly consequences?

"I hope everything works out." Erik remained politely neutral.

"My uncle was a recluse," Carr added. "No one knew where he lived. I might not be able to find all his property to close things out." He sighed. "Guess I'll take it one day at a time."

He gave a wave and then left the shop without buying anything. Erik stared after him, puzzled.

Was he sizing me up to see if I knew anything? Fishing for information? Hard to tell what he knows and what he might have been hoping to learn.

Erik saw Susan motion to him from the break room door and guessed she was asking whether Carr was gone.

"It's safe to come out," he said, laughing. "Were you hiding?"

Susan grimaced. "Not exactly. I just didn't want to talk to that man."

"Why not?" Erik respected Susan's hunches.

"I've seen him outside through the window a couple of times," she confessed. "He stood across the street and stared at the shop like he couldn't decide whether to come in. I was afraid maybe he was casing us for a robbery."

"He looks more like the kind to pick up a vintage watch for his polo instructor," Erik countered. "Interesting that you went right to 'criminal.'"

Susan blushed. "Ignore that. I'm a little jumpy."

Erik shook his head. "I think your instincts are spot on. Jaxon knew him in New York and warned me about him. Ben had a run-in with him as well."

"Do you think he told the truth about why he's in Cape May?" Susan ran her hands up and down her upper arms to warm herself as if she had taken a sudden chill.

"I think he told part of it," Erik said. "I got the sense that he was trying to find out what I knew and not telling me everything that he did. But I'm not sure what to make of that."

"You should tell Cole," Susan prompted. "It will be up to the police to release Raines's belongings."

"Someone also broke into Raines's car," Erik mused. "That happened after the murder. Which would suggest two people are involved. But what is someone looking for? The poker chips can't be that important."

"Are they haunted? If Ben can't read them, maybe Monty can."

Erik grinned. "That's a great idea. I'll talk to Ben about both things tonight at dinner."

They closed the shop, and Erik walked Susan to her door, even though her house was across the street.

"You know I'll be fine on my own," she told him with a pat on the arm.

"Too much strange stuff is going on," Erik said. "Indulge my protective streak."

"Go have dinner with your boy," she told him as she opened the door. "And don't talk shop all night!"

Erik checked the lock and the security system on Trinkets as he walked past, then headed up the steps. Shorter off-season hours now meant that he left and got home from work earlier than Ben, which gave him some extra time for research or to cook dinner.

Tonight, the aroma of braised beef short ribs in red wine rose from the slow cooker. Erik's stomach rumbled. He put the mashed potatoes he had made the night before in the microwave to heat. A bagged salad with shaved cheese and crunchies would make a good side, and he pulled items from the fridge as well as a take-and-bake baguette for crunchy bread. He had already set out one of their favorite cabernet sauvignons before work so he didn't forget.

Needing a break from the day, Erik turned on music, loud enough to keep his thoughts from going over the case. Before he knew it, Ben's key jingled in the lock.

"That smells amazing." Ben took in a deep breath and released it with a pornographic moan.

"Keep that up and we'll be eating dinner cold," Erik joked.

Ben came up behind him at the counter and wrapped his arms around Erik's waist, pressing a kiss to his neck. "Hmm. You smell great too. I think I'll have you for dessert."

"With a cherry on top?"

"I think we both lost our cherries a long time ago."

"Each time we do something new it counts as a whole new cherry." Erik turned to take Ben in his arms and kiss him properly. He felt them both chub.

"That so?"

"I was thinking we could take a bath tonight after dinner, like in that video we watched." Erik kissed him again lightly before turning back to finish the salad.

"The one in New Orleans?"

"Uh-huh."

"That was really hot—but I think their tub was bigger."

"Ours is big enough."

"Any chance of having dessert first?"

Erik shot him a lascivious grin. "Not when the short ribs are done. Go wash up while I get dinner on the table."

Ben gave him a swat on the ass in passing, but went to change out of his work clothes as Erik put salad and dressing at their places, took the bread out of the oven and sliced it, poured water and wine, and then plated the beef and potatoes. On a whim, he used fancier plates than usual, a matched Noritake set he had kept from an auction because he thought they were pretty.

"Is it date night? What's the occasion?" Ben came into the room wearing a T-shirt and a pair of gray sweatpants that made no secret of his arousal.

"Just felt like it," Erik said. "Sit. Eat. Then we can get to dessert."

"A few updates, and then no more business talk," Ben said as he poured dressing on his salad. "I told Cole about the car break-in, and he said he's still waiting on the official autopsy and doing a records search. I guess Raines did a good job of scrubbing his footprints when he went dark."

Erik filled him in on Carr's visit, Jaxon's warning, and Susan's reaction.

"Yeah, you saw that he came to see me, sniffing around," Ben replied. He filled Erik in on everything else he had learned while they were apart. "I agree that there's something about Carr that doesn't sit right. Tomorrow, I'm going to see what my PI resources can pull up and maybe get Teag and Vic involved."

Teag Logan was an expert hacker, while Vic D'Amato was a Myrtle Beach police detective and had access to law enforcement databases that Ben couldn't access legally.

"Susan suggested having Monty take a look at the poker chips," Erik said after a few sips of wine. "Not dissing your ability, but—"

"But you're right. I might see a ghost, if there is one, but if the spirit isn't strong enough to communicate, I don't have the power to help them show themselves. I can call Monty tomorrow and set something up."

Erik nodded. "The sooner the better. I think everything's

connected, but we're missing some pieces, and I'm afraid that's going to come back to haunt us."

"I see what you did there." Ben grinned.

Erik rolled his eyes, but he couldn't help smiling. "I didn't intend to."

"Sure you didn't."

They kept the conversation light for the rest of the meal, enjoying the decadent beef and the excellent wine pairing.

"You spoil me." Ben poured them both more wine. "I was a shot and a beer kind of guy before I met you."

"I like the sound of that—spoiling you." Erik met Ben's gaze with intent. "Not that there's anything wrong with Boilermakers."

"Umm. You've opened my eyes to the finer things in life," Ben said, only half-joking. "I'm glad you were willing to overlook my rough edges. I'm kind of a 'scratch and dent special.'"

Erik took his hand and twined their fingers together. "I love you just the way you are for being exactly who you are. Don't ever doubt that."

They both made a point to stop before they were stuffed so they didn't fall asleep from the rich food and wine. "Why don't you run the bathwater, and I'll put food in the fridge and join you?" He pulled Ben in for another kiss before he turned to the counter.

"Don't keep me waiting." Ben gave Erik's ass a squeeze for good measure.

Moments later, Erik heard water running, and hurried to package the last of the leftovers. He made sure the security system was on, then went to join Ben, shedding his clothing outside the bathroom door.

The smell of sandalwood and orange in the humid bathroom air told Erik that Ben had used one of their bath bombs. The old house didn't have a modern shower, just a shower head over a huge cast iron tub with a curtain. While Erik sometimes missed a modern enclosure, the made-for-two tub that fit both men had its benefits.

Ben moved his legs apart for Erik to nestle between them. As he pressed back against Ben's chest and groin, he felt Ben's hard length.

"Did you start the party without me?"

"I just wanted to be ready to rumble when you got here," Ben told him, reaching forward to run soapy hands down Erik's arms and over his chest, making sure to tweak his nipples on the way.

Erik let his head fall back against Ben's shoulders. "Do that again. Feels good."

Ben chuckled in a throaty voice that went right to Erik's cock. "Oh, I plan on doing it over and over."

Erik turned so he could kiss Ben on the side of his face, mouthing down his stubble-lined jaw. Ben's hands slid down Erik's belly, skirting his cock, and then along both thighs with a light touch.

"Like this?" Ben murmured.

"Uh-huh." Erik slid his hands along Ben's legs, then back to cup his ass and hitch them a little closer.

Ben wriggled, pressing his hard cock against the crack of Erik's ass. "Impatient, much?"

"Still hungry, I guess."

"Mmm. I've got just the thing to fill you up." Ben's hand dropped to Erik's cock and began to stroke him slowly, swiping his thumb over the head and pressing just below the flare to make Erik gasp.

"Want you." Erik had no qualms about taking the lead, but he also enjoyed letting Ben set the pace. Being able to trade off who initiated as well as switching top and bottom just seemed to come naturally, and it was something he valued in their relationship.

"I've got you. Just leave it to me," Ben murmured.

Alarms shrilled, jolting both of them and ruining the mood.

"Shit. That's the store." Erik got to his feet and looked back to Ben. "Sorry."

"Go. Put on pants and get your gun. I'll be right behind you."

Erik hurried to pull on sweatpants and a shirt, foregoing socks. He grabbed his Sig Saur from the kitchen drawer as he headed for the door.

The store's alarm summoned the police, but a thief might be long gone by the time they arrived. Between good locks, the security system, and magical wardings, Erik wasn't worried about someone actually gaining access. What did concern him was why someone tried to break in—and what they were after.

As he feared, there was no one in sight by the time he got to the street. Erik heard Ben thump down the stairs behind him and knew Ben had his Glock in hand.

"Gone," Erik said as a siren sounded in the distance. He went to the panel by the store's entrance and entered the code, silencing the alarm, and then examined the lock.

"Idiot tried to pick it—with a keypad right next to it, so there was no question about a security system," Erik muttered. "Doesn't look like there's any damage."

He and Ben made sure their guns were carefully set aside on the steps and out of sight by the time the squad car pulled up.

"Everyone okay?" Deputy Jeremy Williams knew Ben and Erik on sight and gave them a once-over, probably looking for blood.

"Yeah, we're fine," Erik replied. "Thanks for coming so quickly. It looks like someone tried to jimmy the lock but didn't get very far."

Williams bent over to have a look at the door, then straightened and nodded. "Alarm scared him away before he could do much. That's a good thing. Have you seen anyone hanging around, casing the place?" Thankfully, he didn't seem fazed by the fact that both Ben and Erik had wet hair and had clearly been interrupted.

Erik glanced at Ben and knew they were thinking the same thing. "Holden Carr," Erik said.

"The guy who came to claim the murder vic's body?" Williams asked.

"Just a hunch, but something about the guy seems off," Erik replied. "He stopped in at the store earlier today, and it seemed to me that he was fishing for information more than he was actually shopping."

"He showed up at the rental office today too. I said I couldn't let him take any of his uncle's things until the chief gave the okay," Ben added. "And I had the same feeling Erik did—that he was angling for gossip. It just struck me strange."

Williams grimaced. "Carr's been busy—he was at headquarters too.

Seemed to be in a hurry to get the personal effects from the dead guy. I don't think he made a good impression on the chief."

Erik and Ben sometimes butted heads with Chief Hendricks, but Erik respected the man's ability as an agent of the law.

"I didn't get a look at the perp," Erik confessed. "But if you want to come inside, we can look at the video."

He opened the shop and headed to the monitor in the office. Ben and Williams crowded around him as Erik backed up the recording.

"There," he said as a shadowy form approached. The person kept their head down, and between a ball cap, hoodie, and health mask, the face was hidden. Dark loose clothing made it difficult to judge height, weight, or gender. Gloves meant no fingerprints.

The thief ignored the keypad and tried to pick the lock, then fled. The whole incident took less than a minute.

"Not a pro," Williams surmised, straightening. "An experienced thief would have had a scrambler or a code key for the box."

"Not to mention that he sucked at lockpicking," Ben observed. "Which to me makes Carr even more of a suspect. He might have played a burglar on Broadway, but he doesn't strike me as a B&E type of guy."

"I'd agree, from what little I saw of him," Williams said. "Think he hired someone? That seems more his speed. Maybe they were just testing our system, seeing how long it took for help to arrive."

Erik gave the cop a look. "Is there a directory of Cape May rent-a-robbers? If he came in from the city, how would he know any of the local troublemakers?"

Williams shrugged. "Just tossing out ideas. Your thief might not have known how to break in, but he did know how not to give anything away on the security camera, so he at least anticipated there would be surveillance."

"Sorry to run you out here for nothing," Erik said.

"Livened up a boring shift," Williams joked. "I'll take a look around outside, but if he stuck to the sidewalk, there won't be footprints. Maybe some nearby places have surveillance cameras I can check. And since he didn't break the plate glass window, I think that rules out a smash-and-grab. If he just wanted a quick buck, he'd have gone for anything he could snatch."

"Which means he might have been looking for something specific," Ben added. A glance between Ben and Erik passed a wordless conversation, making it clear they were both thinking about the poker chips.

"Did you get any high-end, really expensive pieces lately?" Williams asked.

Erik shook his head. Whatever the chips were, they wouldn't be attractive to a thief looking to fence the loot for a quick buck. "It's been quiet lately. The last estate sale brought in some nice mid-range items, but nothing particularly rare or expensive—at least, not by the shop's standards of expensive."

Cape May catered to an upscale crowd, so Erik's store wasn't out of line price-wise from the other shops offering quality goods.

"If someone just wanted fast money, it would be a lot easier to sell stuff from just about any other store in town," Ben pointed out. "Pricy purses or jewelry wouldn't be as identifiable. Erik's items are one-of-a-kind."

"Anyone ever tell you that you think like a perp?" Wilson joked.

"Ex-cop. What can I say?"

Erik shivered as water dripped from his hair, soaking the neckline of his T-shirt. Ben stood closer, lending some body heat.

"Alrighty. I'll take pictures and get out of your way," Williams said. "The write-up will be on the chief's desk in the morning. Just in case, be careful and keep an eye out for anything strange."

Williams snapped photos and gave a jaunty wave as they closed the door behind him. Erik re-armed the security system, and he and Ben retrieved their guns before returning upstairs.

By now the bathwater was cold, and the mood was broken.

"Rain check?" he asked as he locked the apartment door.

"Let's get dried off and make out on the couch," Ben suggested. "I'm too wired to try to sleep, and a break-in is an effective cockblocker."

Erik made hot chocolate, and they huddled together on the couch, watching a show on the secrets of Egyptian pyramids that they had seen before. Ben put an arm around Erik's shoulders, and Erik leaned in.

"Thanks for having my back," Erik said quietly.

Ben chuckled. "Did you think I was going to just stay in the tub while you faced the burglar by yourself?"

"No. But I felt better knowing you were behind me," Erik said.

"I had plans to be behind you all along, but it didn't exactly work out the way I fantasized."

Erik tilted his head up. "You fantasized about tonight?"

Ben took a drink of hot chocolate. "Sure. I think about you all the time. Breaks up the workday."

"Beats watching porn at the office."

"My aunt and uncle still own the place and have access to the computer system. So just—no," Ben said with a shudder. "But dirty thoughts don't leave a trace."

"Oh yeah?"

Ben set his drink and Erik's on the end table. "See, I was going to run a nice hot bath, make it smell real good, and get you all worked up in the tub."

"Go on."

"Even made sure I didn't overfill it—like that one time," Ben said, and Erik couldn't help chuckling at the memory of sloshing water on the floor during an early escapade.

"Then I was going to open you up and have us both nice and hard and pull you back to sit on my cock," Ben growled. "Take it slow until you were begging to come."

As he talked, Ben's hand fell between Erik's legs, stroking him through his sweatpants.

"Yeah?"

Ben slipped his hand down Erik's pants a moment before Erik reached for Ben's cock. Erik shifted so the angle made it easier for them to touch.

"Yeah. Just like that," Ben said in a breathy voice as they stroked and pumped.

Erik felt the heat build and blossom, and then he spilled over Ben's fist. Ben followed him seconds later, and they leaned on each other, sticky and sated.

"Not quite the big seduction I had planned, but definitely takes the edge off." Ben pressed a kiss to the side of Erik's head.

"I'd say we both ended up happy." Erik felt warm and relaxed, a big change from the tension of earlier in the evening. "Was it good enough to fantasize about tomorrow?"

Ben laughed, a low, sexy rumble. "Oh, yeah."

Erik pulled his T-shirt off and used it to clean them up. "Come on. Let's go to bed. I'm done with today."

Later, when they lay tangled together, Erik couldn't sleep. Although no harm came of the attempted break-in, he still felt violated by an intrusion into his safe place.

Nothing happened—this time. What if they try again?

If it's Carr, what does he think I might have that he wants that badly? If he thought Raines had anything with him, he'd be breaking into the rental office, not Trinkets. How could he even know about the poker chips? I don't have a clue who sent them, where they've been—or if they actually have anything to do with any of this mess.

Ben snuffled in his sleep and shifted closer. Erik concentrated on the warm body beside him and Ben's scent of sweat, shampoo, and sex.

What if we had caught him? We had guns—did he? Nothing in the store is worth either of us dying over. We should have bolted the apartment door and waited for the cops.

But that's not really what Ben and I do.

I came here to get away from the crazy violence. Ben and I haven't been looking for trouble. How did it find us?

Erik focused on the sound of Ben's breathing, concentrating on matching the rhythm. In, out. In, out.

We're here. Together. Safe. And I'm going to do everything in my power to keep things that way.

After a while, exhaustion won out, and Erik fell into a fitful sleep, one hand resting on Ben's arm for reassurance.

SEVEN

BEN

"**E**verything okay?" Jenny asked when Ben came into the rental office a little late. "You look like you didn't sleep."

"Someone tried to break into Trinkets last night," Ben told her. "We scared him off, but that doesn't make it any less upsetting."

"Did anyone get hurt?"

Ben felt bad about mentioning the break-in because Jenny was the worrying type. Then again, he figured word would be all over Cape May by lunchtime.

"Erik and I are okay. But we don't know who did it or why. Doesn't make for a good night's sleep."

"On the bright side, no one tried to break in here for a change," Jenny pointed out.

"I guess that's something," Ben agreed. "I'm going to do a little private eye work this morning, so please don't let anyone bother me unless it's urgent."

"You got it."

Ben grabbed a cup of coffee and a donut from the break room and then went in his office and closed the door. While his computer powered up he stared at the screen and planned his next move.

He logged into a couple of data bases for private investigators and typed in everything he knew about Holden Carr. Ben didn't have a home address, and New York City was a big place, but he counted on the unusual first name to yield a few hits.

Several pings meant he'd gotten matches on his prompt. Ben watched the results scroll up his screen.

Carr's got money problems. Overdue loans, poor credit score. Late payments. He said he was an actor, but maybe roles have been hard to get now that he's not as young as he used to be. New York's a pricy place to live. Did he get used to expensive tastes when things were good?

Holden Carr's profile revealed a man teetering on the edge of ruin. While he hadn't been in trouble with the law, a couple of notations pointed out Carr's involvement with some dicey business ventures that had come under investigation.

He's heard about hidden treasure all his life, linked to both his great-grandfather and his uncle. Then Tom suddenly shows up. How did Carr know? What did he expect? Was he going to hit Raines up for money? Or did he think that Raines left his hiding place because he'd finally figured out where Edwin hid his famous stash? Was Holden going to try to make a deal with Raines—or take the loot for himself?

Ben weighed which of his friends to call. Vic could access police resources, but Chief Hendricks might decide to share information, and Ben didn't want to go around him unless he had no choice. Teag, on the other hand, had less orthodox connections but might uncover a different sort of evidence.

He decided to wait on the call to Vic and see if Hendricks would play nice. Teag answered on the first ring.

"Great to hear from you, Ben. What's new up north?" Teag teased. Based in Charleston, SC, Teag's weather was almost certainly warmer than Cape May's chilly early autumn.

"Not much. Just murders and mobsters," Ben replied, intentionally off-handed.

"Sounds normal to me. How can I help?"

Ben told Teag about Raines's murder, the poker chips, Carr's unexpected and questionable appearance, and the break-ins at the rental unit and Trinkets as well as their angry ghost and the reluctant spirit at the convent.

"Never a dull day with y'all, is there?" Teag replied. "Wow. Wait 'til I let Cassidy know you're outdoing us in weird spooky stuff."

"Pretty sure it's not a competition," Ben joked. "And there's probably a shitty prize for winning."

"Do you have photos of Tom Raines and Holden Carr? I can run them through some paranormally-enhanced photo matching programs and see if anything turns up. Give me the known aliases for Edwin and Galen Raines, and we might get some more obscure or hard-to-find matches," Teag said.

Teag had magically-enhanced hacking skills given his ability as a Weaver witch. His expertise extended to the Darke Web, the ensorcelled-encryption online underground frequented by people and creatures with paranormal abilities. On the Darke Web, the "ghost in the machine" might really be a ghost, and the "uncanny intelligence" program could be run by a daemon that was actually a demon.

"Already loaded all of that into the secure transfer protocol," Ben told him. "Along with pictures of the poker chips. They've got what we think is a code on them, and we haven't broken it."

"Ooohh," Teag replied. "I love codebreaking! You know this is all catnip to me, right?"

"I was hoping so." Ben was sure Teag's excitement at the challenge would have him diving into the search immediately.

"Deadline?" Teag asked.

"Remember that bad-luck hotel that sits on a dark genius loci site? Our witchy friends say the energy will wax with the equinox. I don't know if that will make things worse, but I'd rather not find out the hard way."

"Crap. That's coming up fast. I'll jump on this today and keep you posted as I find things," Teag told him.

"Thank you. Please give my best to the gang."

"Will do. Talk to you soon," Teag promised and ended the call.

Ben sat for a moment, staring into space as he thought. He turned back to his computer, looking to see if the tracers he had set on Tom

Raines had turned up anything new. He sighed as he scanned the report and saw that, just like before, all leads ended when Raines disappeared, and nothing connected him with Maine.

On a whim, Ben turned to historical databases searching for Edwin Raines.

As a Newark cop, Ben had more up-close experience with mobsters than he ever wanted. He knew how much Hollywood embellished and romanticized the Mafiosi mythos, and understood the difference between fact and fiction.

That didn't make him immune to enjoying a good gangster movie or rule out a secret fascination with the exploits of larger-than-life criminals, especially those from long ago.

"Did Edwin fly under Nucky Johnson's notice because Fun Factory was small potatoes?" Ben mused aloud. "Maybe it got big enough that the Boardwalk guys wanted a piece of the action."

His search turned up a book, *Seaside Syndicate*, written by Michael Castelammare, a New Jersey historian. The book went into details about the Atlantic City Mob of the early 1900s. To Ben's surprise, one of the items mentioned in the synopsis was the unsolved "heist of the decade" involving Edwin Raines.

He downloaded the book and skimmed the contents, focusing on anything to do with Edwin. Galen and Tom fell outside the book's timeline. Edwin was only mentioned in part of one chapter, but that glimpse still provided some interesting details.

Going with his gut, Ben went to the author's webpage and found his contact information. It didn't take much for someone with a PI background to find a phone number.

"Mr. Castelammare? My name's Ben Nolan from Cape May, and I have some new information in the Edwin Raines saga you might find interesting." Ben hoped curiosity would be enough to draw the historian out.

"How did you get my number?"

Ben couldn't blame the guy for being cautious, especially given his subject matter. "I'm an ex-cop from Newark and a private investigator looking into the recent murder of Edwin Raines's grandson, Thomas."

"What do you want?" Castelammare sounded wary, but interested.

"I'd like to spitball theories with someone who knows the Raines family history," Ben replied. "Completely unofficial, totally off the record. I'll keep your name out of it. But you did, after all, write the book on it."

"Ask your questions—I reserve the right not to answer."

Castelammare sounded like a curmudgeon, but Ben wondered how many crank or threatening calls the academic might have fielded over the years. The book wasn't a recent publication or a bestseller. But if it exposed insider gossip, Ben suspected that some individuals might not be pleased, even nearly a century after Edwin's crime.

The Mob prized its privacy and secrets.

"Do you think that Edwin's car wreck was an accident?" Ben led with an easy question since Castellammare had flirted with a theory in the book.

"No. I couldn't come out and say that in the book—my publishers were afraid of lawsuits or maybe of finding a horse's head in their beds," the author replied. "But I don't think anyone at that time thought it was really an accident, and that includes the cops. They just couldn't prove anything."

"Do you think anyone has found Edwin's loot?"

Castellammare took longer to answer. "Are you a treasure hunter?"

"No. But I think someone killed Tom Raines because they thought he found a clue to his grandfather's stash, and I'm trying to keep other people from getting hurt," Ben replied.

"I don't know where it is, and I wouldn't tell you if I suspected anything," the writer said. "Just to get that out of the way. But I don't have any reason to think the money's been found. If a civilian stumbled upon its hiding place, there'd be news coverage. If the Mob recovered it, there would be ripples. I still hear things, on occasion, through my sources."

"The heist was over a hundred years ago. Everyone involved is long dead," Ben pointed out.

"The Mob has a very long memory, Mr. Nolan. If you've done any research, you should know that."

Oh, believe me, I know first-hand. Ben's hand rose to rub the old scars from the bullet wounds that ended his career as a cop and nearly killed him.

"What form was the money in when Edwin took it? Gold? Paper bills? Bearer bonds?" Surely Edwin would be smart enough to steal real money and not house chips that would be completely worthless.

"The fire that night—arson, clearly—caused a lot of chaos, which helped Edwin get away with what he did," Castellammare said. "One of the cashiers at the Fun Factory said that Edwin held up the casino's cage in the midst of the evacuation, shot the guards, and demanded all the 'assets.'"

"I think he picked that night for the heist because there were some Great Gatsby-type high rollers in from New York who were paying in gold and silver," the author confided. "Either he knew what to expect from them, or he'd been waiting for the right time and seized the moment."

"If that's the haul he got, it could still be valuable after all these years," Ben replied. Paper money would turn to sludge if not stored carefully, and stock certificates could become worthless over time. Silver and gold retained their value.

"Exactly. I wrote my theory that Edwin intended to skip the country, so he hid the treasure while he put together what he needed," Castelammare said.

"He probably had a hiding place already picked out because he wouldn't keep the goods on him. We don't know what he did in the time between fleeing Cape May and being killed in the accident. It was only a few days, but he could have gotten a couple hundred miles away on a train and back. The treasure could be anywhere in that radius," the author continued.

Not anywhere. He'd pick a remote location, one where no one was likely to see him hide the goods. Ben made a note to figure out the railroad lines at that time to see if any likely sites jumped out at him.

"Rumor has it that Edwin's son, Galen, was killed not just because he was carrying on the family tradition of skimming money from his employer but because someone thought he might know where his dad buried the loot," Ben suggested.

"If Galen knew, he would have taken the money and set himself up like a king in Mexico," Castelammare said. "He wouldn't have kept working as a low-level accountant. I can believe that Galen looked for the stash, and people watching him decided to take over the search, but I don't think he found anything himself."

Ben had to agree with that logic.

"Galen's son Tom embezzled millions and then vanished for over two decades," Ben said. "Until he turned up dead under an assumed name in a Cape May rental unit. Can you think of any reason Tom would have come out of hiding besides having a credible lead on Galen's treasure?"

Castelammare didn't answer immediately, and Ben thought he might skip the question. "I don't know anything. Don't drag me into this. I've managed not to get killed so far, and I'd like to keep it that way. But...I think your theory is likely. Not that Tom actually did know where to find the money, but he thought he did."

"He probably thought everyone had forgotten about it," Ben mused.

"Like I said—long memories," the author cautioned.

"Just a few more questions." Ben sensed he was running out of goodwill. "Your book had a fascinating chapter about mobster super-stitions, supernatural secret societies, and witches. Do you believe in that sort of thing?"

"Cape May's one of the most haunted places on the Jersey Shore," Castelammare answered. "It's got more ghosts per square foot than anywhere besides Salem and Charleston. Hard to spend time there and not at least wonder."

"We had a case here where the ghost of a mobster's *strega* caused a lot of problems," Ben said, and realized how unhinged that could sound. "Did Edwin cross someone's witch? He worked for the owner of the Commodore Wilson Hotel, which everyone thinks is cursed."

"Rumor has it that the owner of the Commodore Wilson at the time, a guy named Nathan Jepson, asked a big shot in the Atlantic City

Mob for money to help him save his hotel and got turned down," the author replied.

Ben thought about the old plate Erik had set aside and the images it had shown him. *Did he see Jepson get turned down by the Mob, which was the nail in the coffin for Jepson's ownership? Or was the actual incident more violent?*

"Were the Bone Men involved?" Ben asked.

Ben had never seen the term "Bone Men" before Castelammare's book, but he vowed to ask Teag and do some digging. It referenced a cabal of witches, sentient creatures like vampires and werewolves, and ghosts who made up an underground supernatural syndicate.

"If you know what's good for you, leave that alone," the author cautioned, and Ben picked up a note of fear in the man's voice. "Some of them are immortal, or at least, unusually long-lived. They're real, and you do not want to mess with them. You definitely don't want them on your trail."

"So the idea of mobsters being superstitious—it's not just bringing over tales from the Old Country?"

"Those tales were rooted in unholy things they brought with them," Castelammare said. "There's a reason I never wrote the sequel book, which was supposed to be about mafia magic. I can take a hint."

Ben wondered what kind of warning the writer had received to scare him so thoroughly.

"Last question. Was there anyone at the time who would have taken Edwin's betrayal personally?" If they were branching out to look at mafia ghosts, Ben figured he might as well narrow the field.

"Well, his employer at the Commodore Wilson wouldn't have been fond of him," Castelammare replied in a dry tone. "It was rumored Jepson had investors with links to the Mob. Not exactly mobsters themselves, but 'mafia-adjacent.' Business owners who profited from having an 'arrangement' with the Mob without actually getting their hands dirty."

Ben knew the type from his days in Newark. They were complicit but hard as hell to prosecute.

"Anyone else?"

"Nucky Johnson, the mafia king of Atlantic City, was by all accounts a 'gentleman gangster.' He maintained plausible deniability and let his lieutenants handle the rough stuff," the writer said. "If you read the book, you know that my theory was he didn't like there being a casino outside of Atlantic City that he didn't control, and he really didn't like it when it became profitable."

Castelammare cleared his throat. "If you're looking for spurned lovers or double-crossed business partners, I didn't turn any up in my research. Edwin married, but they had one child and were estranged most of the time. Galen also produced a child, but he wasn't exactly a family man either. I never heard that Tom had either a wife or a child."

Ben's eyes widened. "Wait—how many children did Galen have?"

"One, to the best of my knowledge."

"Any credible bastards?"

Castelammare laughed. "Mobsters aren't known for abstinence, but if there were other children linked to Galen, no one mentioned it."

Ben's heart raced. "Thank you. I've taken up enough of your time. By the way, I enjoyed your book."

"Glad you liked it. Now if you would, please lose my number. I'd like to live out the rest of my years in peace."

Ben ended the call, adrenaline surging. *Galen had one child—Tom. Tom didn't have siblings. If there's no brother or sister, he's not anyone's uncle, and Holden Carr isn't really his nephew.*

Thoughts spinning, Ben sent a follow-up email to Teag, saying he needed to know more about the Bone Men.

Ben had some knowledge about mafia witches. He and Erik had tangled with some in the past. It didn't surprise him that organized crime would look to improve their odds of success with a supernatural edge. Dark magic also provided harder-to-trace ways to handle enemies and rivals.

He'd heard others in their friend circle of ghost and monster hunters mention paranormal cartels, but he hadn't needed to pay attention, so the details didn't stick in his memory.

Vampires and werewolves—and some high-powered witches—have longer lifetimes than regular people, verging on immortal. I can imagine that would lead them to protect themselves and their interests using the powers at their disposal. They can afford to play a long game. They also prize privacy and security.

It's not bad enough to have the mortal mafia—now they've got magic and monsters.

His phone chimed, and Ben grabbed it, expecting Teag. Instead, Chief Hendricks greeted him.

"Nolan. We've got the guy who killed your renter. Can you bring your cousin down to the station?"

"Is it Holden Carr?"

"No."

"Carr isn't actually Tom Raines's nephew. Raines didn't have siblings," Ben blurted.

Hendricks was silent for a moment. "Interesting. Come down, and we'll talk. See you *soon.*" His emphasis made it clear he expected a quick response.

Ben sighed and dialed Sean. "Hey. Chief Hendricks says they caught the killer, and he wants us to go down to the station. How soon can you meet me here? I got the feeling Hendricks doesn't want to be kept waiting."

"Give me fifteen. I was packing up to head back to Wildwood," Sean replied.

"You got it." Ben ended the call. He thought about calling Erik and decided to wait until he found out what Hendricks would share about the murder.

If Carr isn't a nephew, who is he? I didn't buy the "long-lost family showing up out of the goodness of his heart" bit, but at least a nephew is a real connection. Bastard son? Tom probably sowed some wild oats before he became a recluse. Cousin on the other parent's side? Or just someone who heard the stories and decided to fake his ID for a chance to find a treasure?

"We've got to go down to the police station," Ben told Jenny when Sean showed up. "Sounds like they might have caught the killer."

"I'll keep everything running while you're gone," Jenny promised.

Ben filled Sean in on what Hendricks had told him as they headed for the station, but kept some of the other things he had discovered to himself for now. Knowledge might be power, but it was also dangerous, and Ben didn't want to put Sean at more risk than absolutely necessary.

Ben and Erik had become reluctant supernatural sleuths and accepted what went with the role. *I'd rather not drag Sean into it. Let him live a normal life.*

Or as normal as you can be selling onion rings in Wildwood.

The officer at the desk waved them through. "Chief is waiting for you in the back."

They hurried toward the briefing room, and it occurred to Ben that perhaps he should be concerned that he knew his way around quite so well. Hendricks was already at the table.

"Come in. I've got questions." Hendricks gestured toward mugshot printouts. "You ever see this guy before?"

Ben and Sean moved closer. The man in the mugshot looked to be in his late twenties or early thirties, unremarkable except for his dead-eye stare.

"Who is he?" Ben asked. "I don't recognize him."

Sean shook his head as well.

"Edward Frazetti, aka 'Freaky Eddie Frazetti,'" Hendricks said with distaste. "He's got a rap sheet longer than my arm, and that's not counting records that were sealed from his stint in juvie."

"Upstanding citizen," Ben observed. "How do you know he killed Raines?"

Hendricks shrugged. "Good old-fashioned police work. Got a tip about an odd man at the coin-op laundry trying to get blood out of his clothing. Put the security and traffic cam photos together and tracked him down, matched the blood to Raines."

"Contract kill?" Ben asked.

"He's not saying anything, but that's my guess," the chief said. "My question is—why did he stick around after Raines was dead?"

A chill went down Ben's spine. "Because that wasn't his only target."

"Bada-bing," Hendricks replied.

"You think he was after Ben—or Erik?" Sean paled.

"Maybe. Tom Raines and his mother moved up the coast after his father was killed. He worked in and around Atlantic City before he disappeared. That means he didn't have a lot of personal ties in town."

Ben thought of the ghost at the convent. She and Raines had fallen out of touch, so she wouldn't have been useful to someone like Frazetti, even if she had been alive.

"But why would the people who sent Frazetti after Raines be interested in Erik or me?" Ben thought hard. "Unless they're still sore about the stuff that happened earlier this year." Unfinished business from both of their pasts had drawn dangerous attention.

Hendricks raised an eyebrow. "You think?"

Ben shrugged. "I kinda figured that would have been sorted out sooner, that's all."

"There's something to be said for giving a mark time to let down their guard," Hendricks replied. "But in this case, I'm working on the suspicion that they think you had proximity to Raines and might have found something or passed something to Erik."

"I didn't."

"Yeah, well. They don't know that," Hendricks responded.

"Then who is Holden Carr, and what's his angle?" Ben asked. "Jaxon knew him years ago in New York City, so he's gone by that name for a long time, but I did some digging and found out Galen Raines only had one child, so Tom wasn't Carr's uncle."

"One *acknowledged* child," Hendricks corrected. "If Carr was talking about missing heist money years ago, like Jaxon told you, he could be Tom's illegitimate child, or the child of one of Galen's bastards if he had any. Whether Carr's a blood relation or not, he's definitely a person of interest, but so far, we haven't caught him."

"You think he's still around?" Sean asked.

"He came here for something—and I don't think he found what he was looking for," Hendricks replied. "That means he probably knows something we don't. And if he was the intruder at Trinkets, then he had a reason to break in. I think he's nearby—and potentially dangerous," he added with a warning glance at Ben.

"You turn up any leads from Frazetti's known associates?" Ben asked. "Odds are good it's someone connected to Tom's embezzle-ment who has a long memory and holds a grudge."

"We're working on it," Hendricks told him. "You're out of the game, Nolan. Leave that to us."

Ben raised his hands in appeasement. "Sure thing. You're getting paid the big bucks."

"How do you manage to be annoying even when you're agreeing with me?"

"Talent," Ben smirked.

Hendricks rolled his eyes. "Thanks for the info on Carr. I don't know that it changes anything, but it might. In the meantime, keep your eyes open and watch your backs. Until we know what they're after, it's going to be hard to get ahead of them."

"Will do," Ben promised, although he was already thinking about running down the occult aspect, which definitely didn't fall under Hendrick's purview.

Sean was quiet as they walked back to the rental office. "What do you make of all that?" he asked after a few blocks.

"I think Hendricks is basically a good guy trying to do his job," Ben replied. "But I also think there's something we're missing, maybe a supernatural angle, that makes sense of all this."

"Do you want me to stay? I can get someone to cover the truck for me," Sean offered.

Ben shook his head. "Thanks, but there's no reason to drag you into this—any further than you already are. Besides, Wildwood's just up the road. I'll call if I need help—promise."

"You'd better," Sean glared.

"I will," Ben swore.

Before he met Erik, Sean was Ben's wingman from the time they were kids. They always backed each other up, and they had shared both secrets and wild times. In many ways, he was more of a brother than his two half-siblings. Ben was happy that Sean had finally escaped Cape May to be living his dream and didn't want to do anything to dent his happiness or his safety. Even so, Sean's offer warmed Ben's heart.

He helped Sean load his car and gave his cousin a side hug. "Drive safely."

"This is New Jersey. Can't promise anything," Sean said with a mischievous glint in his eyes. "Remember—call me."

"Yeah, yeah. Get going. Some of us have to work," Ben grumbled, but the fond tone canceled out his words. He thumped the roof of the car for good measure. "Let me know when you get in."

Sean gave a non-committal wave and drove away.

Ben reached for his phone. "Hey, Monty? I need to ask a favor."

———

Two hours later, after both Trinkets and the lighthouse were closed for the day, Monty Clark met them at the antique shop. Erik made sure to lock the door behind him and turned on the security system.

"Good to see you," Erik said. Ben had known Monty longer, but Erik had forged his own friendship with the park ranger.

"You too. Sounds like you've got something that might have a hitchhiker," Monty replied.

"Come on back," Erik said. Susan had already left for the day, although she had insisted Erik keep his phone handy in case she was needed.

While Erik unlocked the safe, he told Monty about how the poker chips came to be in his possession and the unsettling effect they had on him.

"I can feel a presence too, but not enough to have a conversation," Ben confirmed.

Monty sat at the table and poured the poker chips out of the bag. "Oh, wow," he murmured. "That's one pissed off ghost."

"Will it talk to you?" Ben asked, fascinated to watch his friend at work.

"Yeah. I think she's been waiting for someone who could hear her." Monty closed his eyes and picked up a chip in each hand. Ben guessed the medium was putting himself in a trance so he could better contact the ghost. Whether he would channel the spirit to speak to him depended on several factors, including the ghost's strength and if Monty thought it was safe to attempt.

"Please speak to us," Monty said to the spirit. "We want to know your story and why the chips were sent to the store."

They sat in silence for a moment, and Monty's expression twitched as if he were trying to make out a hard-to-hear conversation.

"Her name is Opal Quinn," he reported.

Erik's eyes went wide, and he caught his breath but didn't interrupt. Ben glanced at his boyfriend, noticing the reaction.

"She says that her mother, Eleanor, was a housekeeper for Edwin Raines. She worked for him for many years, and he was always polite. He said he was going to take a trip and wanted her to keep something safe for him. Said she must keep it a secret and give it to no one but him."

Monty listened a little longer before adding to the story.

"Opal says Eleanor was scared, but didn't want to disobey Edwin. She knew he wasn't a good man, but he treated her well and paid on time. She took the bag home and kept it hidden. Edwin died, and she didn't know what to do, so she kept the chips where they were," Monty continued.

"Before Eleanor died, she passed the burden of protecting the chips to Opal, and in time, Opal passed it to her daughter, Dolores," Monty said. "Dolores didn't have children, and she was getting up in years. She didn't know what to do, and she wasn't sure it mattered anymore since so much time had passed, but she didn't want to have the chips be found by someone after she died, so she sent them to Trinkets."

"Someone broke into Dolores's house a few days ago," Erik said. "Ransacked the place and hit Dolores hard enough to put her in the hospital in a coma. So she can't tell us what she saw."

"Opal saw." Monty's voice had a faraway, sing-song quality that he took on when he conveyed conversations from the spirits.

"Did she see the attacker?" Ben asked. "And did he take anything?"

Monty was quiet again before he raised his head. "Yes, and yes.

Opal says he was a young, handsome man with blond hair. He kept shouting 'where is it?' and he hit Dolores when she wouldn't tell him."

"Carr," Ben snarled. Erik nodded.

"Did Dolores tell him that she had mailed the chips to Trinkets?" Ben asked, more worried than ever for Erik's safety.

Monty shook his head. "No. She just kept pretending she didn't know what he was talking about. That made him angry."

"She should have told him," Erik murmured. "It wasn't worth getting hurt."

Under the table, Ben gave his leg a squeeze in support, knowing Erik felt guilty.

"Opal says Dolores has always been stubborn." Monty chuckled. "Says it runs in the family."

"Does Opal know what the markings on the chips are?" Ben asked. "There had to be a reason why it was so important for Edwin that the chips were kept safe. The casino burned, so the chips themselves didn't have value. Is it a code?"

Monty shook his head. "She doesn't know. Opal only glanced at them once, and she doesn't think her mother ever looked inside the bag. She told Dolores to keep them hidden and not touch them. Opal thought they might be cursed—or haunted."

Erik sighed. "Not exactly in the way she meant, but they might as well have been for all the trouble they've caused."

"Has Edwin's ghost ever showed up?" Ben asked.

Monty hesitated, listening to the ghost. Ben could hear a low whisper, but his gift wasn't strong enough to see the spirit or make out her words.

"No," Monty reported. "Eleanor didn't stay behind either. Opal felt guilty leaving Dolores with the burden since she lived alone. Now that Opal has told her story and the chips are in other hands, she's willing to move on once she knows whether Dolores will wake up or go with her."

"Thank you, Opal, for telling your story," Ben said, and Erik murmured his assent.

"I hope Dolores makes a full recovery," Erik added.

Monty went silent, and his head dipped. For several minutes, he sat very still, taking deep breaths. Finally, he looked up and opened his eyes. "Did you get what you needed?"

Ben nodded. "And more."

"Susan was right that the break-in at Dolores's house had a connection to the murder at the rental unit," Erik said. "I'm so sorry this whole situation hurt her."

"How did Carr find out about the chips?" Ben wondered.

"All it would take is one old rumor," Erik pointed out. "Tom might have been looking longer, but he was hidden away and didn't dare have much contact with people. Carr was on Broadway, dining out on his story about family gangsters and missing treasure. And every time he told his oh-so-entertaining tale, there was a chance for someone to jump in and say, 'well, I heard…'"

Ben blinked. "I hadn't thought about that, but it's genius. Whoever shared the story wouldn't have to actually have proof or know for sure, just pass on the tidbit."

"Over the years, Carr circulated with all kinds of people, while Tom hid on an island in Maine. And Tom still must have uncovered something to make him risk coming out of exile, but he was missing a piece," Erik speculated.

"Or he did know, and 'Freaky Eddie' got to him before he could harass Dolores himself," Ben said.

"I sent pictures of the poker chips to Teag Logan," Ben said. "Teag loves cracking codes. It's like a puzzle for him."

Monty handled the pieces gingerly, although Opal's ghost posed them no harm. Erik reached toward the chits and then withdrew his hand as if burned.

"What's wrong?" Ben asked.

Erik scowled at the pieces like they had bit him. "There's a negative resonance, even after all these years. Not magic or haunted, but… stained."

"You can ask Alessia if she can cleanse the chips when this is all over," Ben suggested. "We might need them the way they are until we've figured this whole thing out."

Erik looked to Monty. "Are the chips dangerous?"

Monty frowned, then shook his head. "I agree with you that the chips have a darkness to them, but it may come from all the death and unhappiness they've been a part of. Opal's spirit intends no harm."

Ben slid a sports drink bottle and a candy bar to Monty to help him replenish his energy. Monty polished both off in record time.

"I'm going to put the chips in the safe until we need them," Erik said. "They'll be protected, and the wardings will cancel their energy." Monty put them back in the bag, and Erik locked it in the safe.

"Thank you," Ben told Monty. "Do you want to join us for dinner?"

Monty smiled. "Thanks for the invitation, but I promised Jon we'd have tacos tonight. He still thinks they're exotic."

Because Monty was a full medium, he could enable his ghostly lover Jon to "cohabit" his body for short periods of time. That included eating, which allowed Jon to taste food and drink through Monty's senses. Back when Jon died, tacos hadn't gone mainstream.

Ben felt certain that Jon and Monty had also found a way to use the cohabiting for more sensual satisfaction but definitely didn't want to know the details.

"Enjoy your dinner then," Ben replied. "A good taco is a thing of beauty."

They walked out with Monty, and Ben stood guard while Erik locked the shop and the outside door.

"Do you want to go out for dinner or stay in?" Ben asked. He thought Erik looked worn.

"I have a take-and-bake pizza in the fridge if you don't mind," Erik replied. "I'm honestly in the mood for 'easy.'"

"I'm always easy," Ben snarked with a lascivious wink. Erik laughed, but it didn't reach his eyes.

"I'll take a rain check on that," Erik replied. "Today's definitely been a mood-killer."

Ben took his hand as they climbed the stairs together, wishing he could say something to make Erik feel better.

As if there wasn't enough underlying stress just getting settled moving in together, we've got a killer on the loose and the rest of this shit going on.

When they got to the apartment, Erik turned the oven on and got the pizza ready while Ben found sodas for now and beer for later.

"You okay?" Ben asked.

Erik shrugged. "Yes and no. I'm glad we found out more about the poker chips. I feel bad for Dolores getting caught up in the Raines's family's mess through no fault of her own. I hope she'll recover."

"She has Opal waiting for her, either way," Ben pointed out as Erik added extra cheese to the pizza. "It's sort of brilliant how Edwin found a way to hide the chips right under the Mob's noses all these years."

"Which makes me wonder—where's the actual money stashed?"

"I'm betting on Teag to figure out those markings on the chips. The question is—does Carr have some other way of finding the location?" Ben took a drink of his Coke and hoped the sugar and caffeine would give him a boost.

"If he's been dabbling with magic or is doing a witch's bidding, the answer is probably 'yes.' So we need to be extra careful," Erik replied.

Ben rose and pulled Erik into his arms. "I'm sorry that things got so crazy. We don't seem to catch a break. When this is over, let's go away for a little bit, spend a long romantic weekend somewhere without ghosts or mobsters."

Erik managed a weak chuckle. "Doesn't that require leaving New Jersey?"

Ben ran a hand through Erik's hair. "Maybe. But we'll go somewhere they're not interested in us."

"I'd really like that."

Ben heard the weariness in Erik's voice. "The timing's been all wrong. I'm sorry if the move made everything worse."

Erik pushed back far enough to look in Ben's eyes. "Are you kidding? It's the only thing saving my sanity, that you're here with me, that we've made this commitment. Just having your things here even if you're not reminds me that I'm not alone."

Ben knew he felt that reassurance, but part of him had been afraid to hope that Erik did too. "Being with you makes me happy. Home is with you." He gave Erik a gentle kiss just as the oven timer dinged.

"Go ahead and put the pizza in." Ben reluctantly let go. "I'm starving."

The pizza was as good as it smelled and he and Erik polished it off. They took the beers into the living room and turned on the television, not really caring what they watched. The series on ancient architecture continued, comfortable background noise and an uncomplicated distraction. Ben sat sideways on the couch so that Erik was between his legs lying back on his chest, but neither of them made an attempt for more intimacy, just glad to be together.

Two beers later, they both were nodding off. Ben pressed a kiss to Erik's temple. "C'mon, sleepyhead. I can't carry you to bed. Let's get some sleep and make a fresh start tomorrow."

Erik let Ben guide him to their room and they fumbled through getting undressed and cleaning up before collapsing into bed. Ben thought the mattress had never felt more comfortable, and he suspected Erik was even more spent.

"Hang in there," he said quietly, not sure Erik was even awake to hear him. "We'll get to the bottom of this. I promise I'll keep you safe."

As he drifted off to sleep, Ben hoped with all his heart that he could keep his vow.

EIGHT

ERIK

The sharp tang of pine surrounded Erik, and a brisk wind made him shiver. He looked around, deep inside an unfamiliar forest, searching for Ben.

Panic fluttered in his chest, and his lungs burned as he took rapid breaths of the cold air. He felt dark power rising around him, prickling his skin and making his hair rise.

Erik didn't need to be a medium to know the forest held its share of ghosts and that he had attracted their attention. Gray figures flitted between the trees, circling as if sizing him up, waiting to make a move.

In the distance, Erik heard running footsteps crashing through the brush. Friend or foe? He wasn't sure and reached for the gun in his waistband.

A shot rang out, loud in the silence of the forest. Erik stumbled, biting back a cry of pain. He felt blood start down his left arm where the bullet grazed him. He dodged behind a tree, searching for his attacker, still trying to make sense of what was going on—

"Erik! Wake up, babe," Ben coaxed. "You're safe. We're home. C'mon—wake up."

Erik groaned as the scene around him faded. His head throbbed. "Vision," he managed.

Ben's worried gaze told him that his reaction hadn't been quiet. "Okay. I'll get you something to drink, and we can talk later."

Erik's right hand went to touch his left arm but came away without blood. "I got shot—"

"We're going to keep that from happening," Ben promised. "I'll be right back."

He returned moments later with orange juice and a cookie. "Here. Take your time."

Erik accepted the glass and snack and ate carefully, trying not to have the food come back up. Ben waited in silence, not rushing him. Finally, Erik gave back the glass.

"Sorry. I keep doing this."

Ben set the glass aside. "No apology necessary. And it was a nightmare the last time, not a vision. Shit happens. What did you see?"

Erik thought for a moment, trying to focus on the images. "I was lost in a pine forest. Didn't know where you were. Then I heard someone running and a gun fired. The bullet grazed my arm."

As he spoke, his right hand came up to cover the place where he'd been wounded. "I hid. I didn't get to see who was after me. That's when the vision ended."

Ben held his hands. "Do you think it was the Pine Barrens?"

"Could be. They'd be close enough that Edwin might have been able to get there to hide his treasure."

"Well, that's more than we knew before."

Erik stared at him. "The Barrens have over a million acres. That's looking for a needle in a pine forest."

"Okay, but it's a direction," Ben replied. "It makes sense Edwin would hide his loot somewhere that wouldn't be easy to find and also wouldn't change much. A building could be sold or torn down. The Barrens are pretty wild, so as long as he could find the spot again, odds were good nothing would have been built or torn up."

"The code on the poker chips—do you think it's coordinates?" Erik felt like his brain was slowly coming back online.

"Probably—but they didn't look like any coordinates I've seen, so I bet Edwin encoded them somehow. That's where Teag comes in. He'll figure it out."

Visions usually left Erik wrung out, unlike the jitters he got from other bad dreams. Ben pushed his hair back from his face and tenderly touched his cheek.

"You need your sleep, and there's nothing to be done right now. Maybe we'll hear from Teag in the morning."

Ben pulled Erik down with him, cocooning them in the soft sheets, close enough to warm Erik and calm him with his presence.

"Thanks for putting up with me, even though I'm weird," Erik mumbled.

Ben pressed a kiss to the back of Erik's neck. "I like your kind of weird. Go to sleep."

Erik meant to protest, but he was asleep before he had the chance.

———

The next morning, Erik nearly had to shoo Ben out of the apartment to get him to go to work.

"I'm fine. Really. Go. You've missed enough work because of this whole situation," Erik said, sending Ben off with a kiss.

Erik finished his coffee and a piece of peanut butter toast and checked the security cameras for the hallway and the front and back first-floor doors. He breathed a sigh of relief to see the areas empty.

He filled a thermos with the rest of the coffee and locked up, going down early to the store. Susan wasn't due in for a few minutes, so Erik had time to finish his first round of coffee before he made a fresh pot.

The bag of garbage in the break room was overflowing, a testament to them being off their regular routine. Erik tied it closed and went out the back door. Just as he was about to swing the bag into the dumpster, he heard the click of a gun's safety.

"Give us what's in the safe, and you don't die," a voice growled behind him.

Erik swung the heavy garbage bag around and to the right,

gambling that the gunman wasn't left-handed. The bag pushed the man's arm out and away from Erik so that the shot went wild.

A second goon emerged from behind the dumpster as the first man struggled to find his footing. Erik's prior work with Interpol had included self-defense training since he exposed the crimes of oligarchs and narco lords.

He wheeled, sending the second assailant sprawling with a kick to the groin, then came up with his own gun drawn and squeezed off a shot just as the first man raised his weapon.

Erik's bullet caught the goon in the shoulder. He backed into the doorway of the shop and slammed his hand against the panic button on the keypad, which set off alarms.

Just in case no one heard the gunshots.

He guessed that if Susan had arrived, she'd had the good sense to stay inside and that the security monitoring service had called the police. The attackers ran off minutes before Chief Hendricks and his deputy roared up in a squad car.

"Two men—went that way." Erik pointed in the direction the goons had fled.

"Stay here," Hendricks ordered. "Mom's got an ambulance coming." He and the deputy returned to their squad and drove off.

The ambulance squealed to a halt at the curb. By now, people had come to the windows and doorways of the surrounding shops and homes. Erik had the presence of mind to put his gun back in his waistband, glad that he had been concerned enough to bring it with him.

"Are you hurt?" The EMT looked Erik over from head to toe.

Erik shook his head. "No, but I shot one of the attackers in the shoulder, so he might need assistance if the cops catch him." He wondered if there would be enough of a blood trail to lead them to the assailant.

Ben showed up seconds later, red-faced and out of breath after running from the rental company. "Susan called."

"I figured."

"She's at the store entrance, sending gawkers on their way." Ben gave Erik a worried once-over.

"I need to send her on vacation and buy her flowers when this is over." Erik felt the adrenaline drop now that he was safe. He had come outside without a coat and started to shiver.

He permitted the EMTs to check him, although he didn't expect to even have a bruise. *It could have been so much worse.*

"I clobbered one guy with the garbage, kicked the other in the 'nads, and then shot the first one when he was drawing down on me," Erik said when the technician put a blanket around his shoulders.

"Did you recognize them?" Ben asked.

Erik shook his head, knowing that Ben wondered if Carr had been part of the attack. "No, but they didn't look like vagrants. I think they were professionals."

When the EMTs released Erik, he and Ben went into the shop. By then, Susan had dispersed the crowd and come inside, still leaving the sign on the door flipped to "Closed."

"Erik—are you okay? I can handle things if you need to go to the hospital," she said, triaging Erik with a glance.

"Thanks, but I'm fine," Erik protested. "Assuming my heart rate ever slows down. I fought them off."

"My boyfriend's a badass," Ben said with pride.

"More like a dumbass, taking on a guy with a gun," Erik admitted. "Fortunately I brought my own gun with me, or it could have gone completely wrong."

"Especially if they were hired goons," Ben added.

Erik shrugged. "So were the guys I trained to fight when I worked with Interpol. The thing is, they tend to underestimate you if you aren't in the organized crime world. I mean, who would expect a museum guy to know how to fight or shoot a gun?" He managed a wan smile.

"I wouldn't know about that. Everyone seemed to expect me to start a brawl from the time I was a kid," Ben said.

"Okay—you do rock the tough guy look, and this is New Jersey— just sayin'," Erik teased.

"Yeah, yeah. Stop dissing my state."

"Wouldn't dream of it."

"Boys!" Susan broke up their banter, grinning broadly. "There's someone at the door who would like a word with you." She pointed to the front window, where a grumpy looking Chief Hendricks waited outside.

"Might as well get it over with." Erik suspected the chief had stern words about the shooting.

"I mean, shoot one guy in an alley, and everyone gets bent," Ben teased.

"Hush," Erik replied.

"I'll go make coffee." Susan excused herself to the break room.

Erik opened the door and stepped back for Hendricks to enter. Ben moved closer, signaling support.

"Did you catch them?" Erik asked.

Hendricks shook his head with a disgusted curl to his lip. "No. Although the blood trail held up for a while. Do you usually carry a piece when you take out the trash?"

"I didn't used to, but maybe I should after today." Erik got the feeling Hendricks's annoyance was over not finding the goons and not directed at him.

"Given how trouble follows you two—and with all the right paperwork and permits in place—maybe that's not a bad idea," Hendricks admitted. "Did you recognize the guys who jumped you?"

"No. They didn't look familiar."

Hendricks pulled out a notebook. "Okay, take it from the top. Give me the whole story."

The chief took notes as Erik recounted what happened, including his glance at the cameras before going out.

"They knew to keep out of sight," Erik said. "I guess they planned to bide their time. I don't know if they intended to shoot me or kidnap me, but I didn't want to find out." He didn't mention the poker chips since they weren't part of Hendrick's investigation, and Erik didn't want them confiscated.

"You think they were connected to the Raines killing?"

Erik nodded. "I don't believe much in coincidence. Either the guys who sent Tom's killer or Holden Carr decided to play rough. But if they thought I had something that belonged to Tom, they're wrong. I don't."

Technically, that was true. The chips were stolen by Edwin and didn't actually belong to anyone in the Raines family.

"I guess that an antique shop would be a likely place to look for something related to Edwin's heist from back in the day," Hendricks said.

"Any chance you might pick up footage of the assailants on the traffic cams?" Erik felt certain Ben's question was timed to change the subject.

"Already requested them for a six-block area," Hendricks answered. "And we've posted a reward for information. We were able to get a blood sample, so that can help make an ID when we have suspects in hand. Gunshot wounds have to be reported, so if the guy you hit turns up in a hospital, we'll know."

"If he's a pro, he won't," Ben said. "There's a whole off the grid underground network out there for patching up hired muscle."

Hendricks gave him a side-eye look. "Your knowledge of the criminal element is impressive, Nolan. Try not to join the Dark Side."

"I'll do my best, but they have cookies," Ben deadpanned.

"You think Holden Carr hired the attackers?" Hendricks asked.

Erik shrugged. "Who else? You've got 'Freaky Eddie' in custody. The people who sent him after Tom have more reason to set their mutts on Carr than on me. Carr's the one actively looking for the heist money. Unless the hit on Tom was for old grudges and had nothing to do with his granddad's hidden treasure."

"Guess we won't know until we catch them." Hendricks snapped his notebook closed. "That's it for now, gentlemen. I'll call you down to the station if we get any leads. And there will be paperwork over you shooting the goon." He paused and looked past Erik. "Don't think I didn't know you're in the back, Mom. Thanks for calling it in."

"This is why I have the scanner," Susan said from the break room, and Hendricks chuckled, admitting she'd gotten the best of him.

"Try not to have a shootout in the street, okay?" he said. "Again, I'll let you know if we find out anything."

By the time Hendricks drove away, all the evidence of the morning's excitement was gone. Erik flipped the sign in the window to "Open."

"Thanks for checking on me. You'd better get back to the office," he told Ben, although he had a crazy desire to lock them both in the apartment until the current danger blew over.

"Yeah, I know. Just—be careful." Ben leaned in and gave Erik a peck on the lips. "I need you to be safe."

"Same here." Erik returned the kiss. He watched Ben leave and slumped against the counter with a heavy sigh.

"Coffee makes everything better." Susan pressed Erik's favorite mug into his hands, filled with brew he could tell had been made from the "expensive" grounds they saved for special occasions.

"You didn't get hurt. That's a reason to celebrate." Susan toasted him with her mug.

"I know you want to keep me safe, and that's why you don't tell me some things." Susan leaned on the counter beside Erik and stared at the window as she talked. "But I'm a grown-ass woman, and I can take care of myself. It's entirely up to you what you decide to share, but I'm a pretty damn good partner when I know what's going on."

Erik felt color rise to his cheeks. "I'm sorry. You're absolutely right. I think the whole 'protect your mom' thing kicks in for both Ben and me."

She rolled her eyes. "Stop it. I get enough of that from Cole. I think he'd roll me in bubble wrap and lock me in a panic room if he could get away with it. I understand—but it's infuriating, and a little insulting, too."

"I think Ben and I have just dealt with really bad people enough times that we don't want people we care about getting hurt again," Erik confessed. "We've both seen the scum at the bottom of the barrel."

"Understandable. But overkill. Now...what's up that you haven't told me?" She grinned.

Erik filled her in on the poker chips and Monty's session with Opal's ghost. He remained vague about the leads Teag was researching due to the questionable legality involved.

"So we were right about there being a connection between that poor woman's home invasion and the case," Susan said. "How awful."

"We can't get a statement from her unless she wakes up, but I'd bet money Holden Carr was the one who attacked her," Erik said. "I hope there's security on her hospital room."

"I'm sure Cole took care of it," she replied, and Erik felt certain that she'd be following up with her son as soon as she was out of earshot.

"Um, just so you know...we didn't tell Chief Hendricks about the poker chips," Erik warned. "They aren't part of the Tom Raines murder investigation, and I have a feeling we're going to need access to them to stop Carr and find the missing money—which we can't do if they're in the evidence locker."

"I agree. It's on a need-to-know basis and might just muddy the investigation," Susan said with a conspiratorial wink.

"Exactly." Erik appreciated Susan's support.

He checked his phone and found several missed messages from Alessia. He went to refill his coffee and returned the call.

"Are you hurt?" Alessia asked. "I heard about what happened."

After the anonymity of living in London and Atlanta, the small-town grapevine of Cape May was both a godsend and a surprise.

"Wow—news travels fast. Yes, I'm safe. What's up?"

Either Alessia took him at his word, or her magic verified his answer because she didn't press the point. "I just wanted to remind you about the ritual tomorrow night at the old hotel site. I know you're not a witch, but the energy is strengthened whenever like-minded souls with abilities show up in support."

"I'll be there, and I doubt Ben will let me go alone," Erik replied. "What do we need to bring, or how do you want us to prepare?"

"You won't actually be doing the ritual, just observing and adding supportive vibes," Alessia told him. "You'll be relieved to know we aren't wearing robes or going skyclad."

"That would be chilly," Erik agreed.

"The things we suffer for our craft," she replied with an exaggerated sigh. "Eat enough to have something on your stomach, but not anything heavy in case the energy makes you queasy. Hydrate. Try to be in a positive, receptive mindset and don't focus on fear or negativity."

She paused. "Given what happened that last part might be rough for you. It's okay if you need to cancel."

"No—I think I'll be fine. It's not like it's the first time I've gotten jumped."

"Wow. I guess that's a positive way of looking at it," Alessia responded. "I'll let you decide that for yourself. We'll have enough people if you are uncomfortable, but we'd welcome your support if you feel up to it."

"What else?" Erik's intuition told him he needed to be at the ritual, regardless of circumstances.

"People may or may not hold hands. They definitely won't sing Kum-Ba-Yah," she added in a dry tone. "An elder will speak the binding spell and then lead the group in a chant. We'll already have sigils marked beforehand, so the active part is pretty quick. Raising the energy is important, and the leader will decide how long the chant goes on and whether to add additional spells depending on how the power feels."

"And afterward we go somewhere for coffee and cookies?" Erik joked.

"I think you have us confused with the Lutherans," Alessia snarked.

"Maybe so," Erik said with a laugh. "I'll see you there."

Fortunately, the rest of the day stayed quiet. Susan polished silver in between customers, and Erik worked on the decidedly non-haunted inventory pieces as time permitted. He breathed a sigh of relief when closing time came.

"Guess we got all the excitement over early." Susan gathered her purse and jacket from behind the counter.

"Excitement is overrated." Erik put on his jacket to walk Susan to her door. Today, she didn't try to talk him out of the gesture, seeming to understand that he needed to make sure she was safe after the morning's danger.

"Try not to dwell on things," she told him as she turned the key in the lock. "You'll feel better in the morning."

Erik knew she returned the protective vigilance by watching from her window until he was back to his door. He waved in acknowledgment, and then ducked inside, setting the alarm and lock on the outer door even though he doubted Ben was home yet. Ben had the key and the code, and Erik felt better with as many precautions in place as possible.

As he had guessed, Ben was still at work. Erik put a frozen beef stew in the oven, not having the spoons to worry about fixing a meal from scratch.

He lit candles in cedar, cinnamon, and clove scents, letting the calming and purifying fragrances fill the air. Then he took a silver chalice down from the cupboard and reached for the small bags of dried herbs Alessia had given him, selecting basil, angelica root, and poplar to add to the cup. He spoke the words of blessing the witch had taught him, then dropped a match into the chalice.

The ingredients sent up an aromatic cloud. Erik closed his eyes and breathed deep, letting the protective smoke waft over him, turning to expose all sides of his body. Between the candles and the burning herbs, the scents soon filled the apartment.

When the herbs burned to ashes, Erik set the chalice in the sink and carried the candles with him to the bathroom. He stripped out of what he was wearing and tossed it in the laundry, pulling out fresh clothes that smelled of lavender.

Erik ran a hot shower and reached for a special bar of soap he kept for occasions where he felt desperate for cleansing that went beyond sweat and dirt. The eucalyptus and mint soap from Alessia's store carried a hint of extra energy in it as well as her blessing. A tingle of positive magic eased his soul.

He lingered in the shower, breathing in the warm, moist air and letting the protective scent of the soap fill the curtained enclosure. He could almost feel the tension and negative resonance from the attack washing away, replaced by a sense of well-being and an awareness of safety.

He wasn't a witch, but Alessia had assured him that not all rituals required special training or more energy than his abilities provided.

"Psychic powers are a type of magic, after all," she had told him. *"We can all do different things, but the energy rises from the same root."*

Feeling much better, Erik ended the shower, toweled off, and got dressed. Then he made a cup of green tea with ginseng, trying to reset from the inside out. He closed his eyes and repeated one of the centering mantras Alessia had taught him, a short phrase that helped him concentrate and keep his thoughts from spiraling.

His phone rang, and Erik realized he had completely lost track of time, having fallen into a light trance.

"I didn't know what headspace you were in, so I thought I'd let you know I'm turning off the alarm to come in," Ben warned him. "Didn't want to worry you."

Ben's thoughtfulness made Erik smile. "Thank you. I've been trying to let go of the day."

"So it's going to smell like the bath bomb shop at the mall?'

"Afraid so, but I'm much calmer now," Erik replied with a smile.

"Then it's worth it. See you in a minute."

Erik had started to set the table and pour drinks by the time Ben hurried inside.

"Smells good." Ben took a deep whiff and smiled.

"Beef stew," Erik replied.

Ben shook his head. "No. I mean, that too. But you, the apartment —smells like home."

He interrupted Erik's dinner preparations to pull him into a full-body hug. "I'm glad you're okay." Ben held Erik tight. "When Susan called me, all she knew was there were shots fired. I was so scared, imagining all kinds of possibilities. Please don't get killed."

Erik felt tears well in his eyes and returned Ben's bear hug. He heard the worry in his boyfriend's voice and felt him shaking.

"I'll do my best not to," Erik promised. "I'm okay. Not even a scratch."

"This time."

Erik ran a hand up Ben's neck and through his hair. "One day at a time is all we get. And I definitely have plans to spend all of mine with you." Erik kissed Ben when they stepped apart and cupped his cheek with his hands. "Let's eat. We'll both feel better."

As they ate, Erik told Ben about Alessia's call and the plans for the ritual.

"Hell, yes, I'm going," Ben said. "I'm glad you realized that."

Erik smiled. "I figured you'd want to be there."

"Someone has to watch your back when you're doing all the witchy woo-woo," Ben replied, taking another bite. A bag salad, frozen loaf of garlic bread, and a good bottle of red wine made the last-minute freezer casserole a hearty dinner, one of Erik's favorites.

"Do you think Holden Carr will show up at the ritual?" Ben asked when they were nearly finished. His plate and salad bowl were empty, and he nibbled his third slice of bread as he toyed with the wine left in his glass.

"I wouldn't be surprised," Erik replied. "I intended to let Chief Hendricks know."

"What's in it for Carr?" Ben mused. "There's no reason to think he's a witch, although he might have a witch helping him. So what would going to the ritual do for him?"

Erik took a sip of his wine before replying. "He shows up just at the time Tom comes out of hiding. He always bragged about his occult interests and 'connections.' His whole joke about 'making a deal with the devil' for his success isn't funny in retrospect. What if he did make a bargain with a witch who knew his connection to Edwin Raines, and retrieving the treasure is his long-due repayment?"

Ben's eyebrows rose. "There are a lot of intuitive leaps in that sentence. Hell, you damn near pole vaulted across a ton of 'what ifs' to get to that conclusion. But…it's worth considering."

"We still don't know who sent Frazetti after Tom, or sicced the goons on me," Erik went on. "But it's interesting that they're not hunting down Carr too."

"That we know about," Ben pointed out. "If Hendricks knew where

Carr was, he'd have brought him in for questioning. If we're going for wild-ass theories, how's this? Carr made a deal with a witch, and now he owes the heist money to pay his debt. The witch alerted him to Tom coming to Cape May, but Tom died before Carr got to him. Carr had some inkling about Edwin leaving clues and knew his connection to the Quinn family, but not what the object was. But he's got an ace— or thinks he does. The witch gave him some sort of object—a relic of some sort—to help him do—I don't know—something."

"If Carr has any hint of abilities, he's got to feel the waxing energy of the genius loci for the equinox," Erik theorized. "There are all kinds of locator spells and objects that help find missing objects. Maybe Carr wants to 'juice up' himself and his special relic to look for the treasure, like a dowsing rod."

"That's a hell of a theory based on almost nothing." Ben took the last sip of his wine. "You realize that, right?"

"Of course. And yet—it's not entirely improbable," Erik conceded. "Carr showed up here with suspicious timing. He's always been connected to the occult—and drawn to darker power. The 'magical mafia' or whatever we're calling them, had previous connections with the Raines family. Carr knew enough to seek out the Quinns."

He paused until a car stopped honking. "We're taking factual points and spinning a theory to connect them. That's what they do in every detective show I've ever watched."

Ben rolled his eyes. "Yeah, well those TV detectives have a script writer working for them to make sure they find all the clues. Real life usually isn't that tidy."

"Still," Erik countered, "it's like putting pins in a map. Start with what you know for certain, connect the dots, and see what you can figure out from the results." In the distance, a dog barked, and Erik glanced out the window to make sure no one was nearby.

Ben tipped his chair onto its back legs. "Okay, I'll play your game. Maybe his relic led him to the Quinns, but he was in the wrong place. What if he thought his Hand of Glory, or whatever the fuck he has, would find the treasure in the Quinn's house, and instead, it just pointed him to where the key used to be hidden?"

Erik nodded in agreement. "So he decides to try again—by following us. But he wants to be ready, and he gets wind of the Commodore Wilson nexus. Maybe he's known about that all along since Edwin worked for one of the guys who owned the hotel. And he thinks that if he gets a power boost and levels up, he'll be able to find the treasure. And somehow he discovers we have something in our safe."

"This sounds like a bad video game," Ben replied.

"It's all speculation, but it's not bad for a working theory since we don't have anything else to go on. And while it might explain Carr's actions and his thinking, it doesn't change our next steps. We still go to the ritual, expect another attack or at least a sighting, and try to make sure when we find out more about the code on the poker chips that Carr doesn't follow us."

Erik's phone rang, and he frowned as he looked at the number. "Hendricks," he mouthed before he answered and put the call on speaker phone.

"Mitchell—we found where Carr's been staying, and I need you and Nolan to make sense of what's here. It's like something out of the *X-Files*."

"I'm guessing that Carr's still at large?"

"Yeah. He must have realized we were closing in because he left most of his stuff and that fancy sports car too," Hendricks replied. "How soon can you take a look? I can text you the address."

Erik exchanged a glance with Ben, who nodded. "We can leave now."

"Good. I just sent you the address. Be careful—we flushed Carr out of his bolthole, but I have the feeling he hasn't left the area."

"Hendricks sounded a little weirded out," Ben said as they drove to the hotel. "That can't be a good sign."

He pulled up in front of a mid-price chain hotel on the edge of town. "It's not a no-tell motel by any means, but I'd expect something fancier for a guy who drives a spiffy car and wants everyone to believe he's a star."

"A lot of things about Holden Carr don't hold up when you look closely," Erik replied.

Hendricks and his deputy were waiting when they arrived. "Glad you came. I know better than to dismiss what's in there as mumbo-jumbo, but it's not what they taught me at the academy."

"Did you touch anything?" Erik asked, worried.

"No. Give me some credit. I watch enough spooky shows on TV to know that's a bad idea. Just took pics of everything."

"Any cold spots? Strange smells?" Erik pressed.

Hendricks shook his head. "Other than incense? No. And we didn't notice that anywhere was colder than the rest of the room."

"Okay—let's see what Carr left behind," Erik said.

Ben and Hendricks followed him while the deputy remained outside on guard.

Erik hesitated at the doorway, scanning the frame for sigils or evidence of spell work, but found nothing. Hendricks pulled the curtains to let in light, and Erik's eyes grew wide.

"Oh, my," Erik murmured.

"Fuck," Ben said beside him.

Old photos, newspaper articles, and newer printouts were taped to the walls around the room. Ink-scrawled sheets of notebook paper littered the floor. Take-out containers overflowed the garbage can.

"Over there." Ben nudged Erik and pointed to the corner.

One nightstand had been moved from the bed to the far wall and served as a shrine covered with a yellow and red cloth. A vase filled with drooping gladiolas in the same colors shared the space with white pillar candles and an incense burner. White ribbons spattered with red trailed from the vase. A figurine of a wolf sat next to the candle.

A few cookies and a withered apple lay on a plate—*probably offerings*, Erik thought. His eye was drawn to an ornate filigree box with a red velvet lining that lay open—and empty—on one side of the table.

On the wall above the shrine hung a poster in the style of a traditional saint's painting. A woman with a defiant expression held a key in one hand and a single red gladiolus stem in the other. Thirty-two bullet holes marked her bloodstained old-fashioned nun's habit.

Erik looked to Ben. "You grew up Catholic. Which saint is that?"

Ben shook his head. "First off, I flunked my catechism. Second—there are hundreds of official saints, not to mention the unofficial ones. And considering everything else we know about Carr, I'm going to bet she's one of the underground saints."

"Underground saints?" Hendricks asked.

Ben nodded. "Ever heard of Santa Muerte? She's a cross between the personification of Death and the Holy Mother—revered in narco culture, along with several other 'unofficial ' saints. The Mob has its own, either saints who aren't acknowledged by the Vatican or traditional saints who have been given a second meaning by the mobsters and the priests who support them."

"Religious mobsters?" Hendricks questioned.

"Did you never watch *The Godfather*?" Ben half turned to give Hendricks the side eye. "The religious ties and rituals run deep, even for the worst of the worst. At least that's true in the Italian Mob."

"Learn something new every day," Hendricks said. "So you think all this means something?" He gestured to encompass everything from the scribbled notes to the shrine.

"Definitely," Erik said. "May I take photos of the shrine? I have contacts who know more about some of these things than I do. But I'm certain there's a reason for this particular saint."

"Go ahead—just don't post it on social media," Hendricks muttered.

Ben made a slow circle of the room, reading the information tacked up on the wall. "He was definitely stalking Tom Raines." He pointed to grainy photos of the dead man.

Erik tore his gaze away from the shrine long enough to glance at the pictures and realized that Carr had made the connection to Fun Factory with antique photos that he probably found online and a newer shot of the tower, all that remained of the old entertainment complex.

Since the tower was now on land used as a military installation, Erik wasn't counting on it being a likely hiding place for Edwin's loot.

"He's got photos of Trinkets too." Ben's voice went flat and cold, something Erik thought of as going into "cop mode," which Ben did when a threat arose. "And some of Tom Raines in the rental unit before the murder."

"Anything else you make of all this?" Hendricks asked.

"Just a theory that Carr got help from a witch with Mob ties to help him track Tom Raines and look for Edwin's treasure," Erik said. "He clearly believes in the supernatural and that it can intervene on his behalf. That makes it likely he trusts the witch as well, and probably has been using spells and rituals to help him search for the treasure."

Erik pointed to the empty filigree box. "That worries me. I think he's gotten his hands on a relic from this saint, something he believes has magical power—and which just might."

"Relic?" Hendricks asked.

"Something that belonged to a saint or biblical figure," Ben clarified. "Nearly all Catholic churches have some sort of relic. It could be a splinter from the 'true' cross or a piece of cloth or a lock of hair from a saint—or a bone."

"Real bones?"

Ben nodded. "It's hard to explain if you don't grow up with it, but that's very common."

"People become saints because they've done something extraordinary, and then people attest to the saint causing miracles," Erik added. "Carr was devoted to this particular saint because he saw a way to get something he wanted. And leaving aside dogma, some relics do possess supernatural abilities. So if he's got a relic, we can be sure he thinks it will help him find Edwin's treasure. He hasn't succeeded yet, though, or I wouldn't have been attacked this morning."

Hendricks pinched the bridge of his nose. "Haunted, religious, supernatural bones. Just when I think things can't get any weirder. Okay—how does all this help us catch Carr?"

Ben wandered around, looking at the papers on the floor without touching anything. "It would help if we could get copies of the maps he's got strewn around. We don't know if he figured out anything about the money's location, but it's clear he sure was trying. It might give us a clue to where we should look—and, at the least, where he'll be looking."

Hendricks nodded. "I can do that. Anything else?"

"Honestly, I'd suggest asking Alessia Mason to check over the room to make sure there aren't any bad magical surprises," Erik said. "You don't have to believe in the paranormal to take precautions. It beats ending up with a bad rash—or being turned into a newt."

"I'll take that under consideration," Hendricks replied. "Anything else?"

Erik glanced at Ben and then shook his head. "Not right now. If you find something you can't explain, ask, and I'll see what I can find out for you. Thank you for calling us in to look at this."

"You're my go-to guys for woo-woo," Hendricks said. "I'm counting on your discretion. I do not want to hear about 'satanic shrines' at the coffee shop tomorrow."

"We don't want that sort of thing going around either," Erik assured him.

Hendricks followed them out and locked the door. "When you find out something about that saint, let me know."

"Will do," Ben said.

Erik and Ben got into their car, and Ben immediately reached for his phone. "I want to send the photos to Teag and see what he comes up with."

"I already copied you on the shrine," Erik told him. "I'm curious myself—and this adds a whole new wrinkle."

"Yeah. Like there wasn't enough going on." Ben sent his message and then started the car and aimed toward home.

When they got back to their apartment, Erik insisted they both change out of the clothes they had been wearing and shower with cleansing herbs to wash away any psychic residue and reduce their tension. Even though the showers were quick and functional, Erik felt much better afterward.

They cleaned up the dishes, and Ben made popcorn. Erik cued up a shark attack movie they hadn't seen yet and gathered extra pillows and blankets to nest on the couch. Ben turned off the lights and made sure the sound settings were ready for dramatic movie music before he and Erik cocooned.

Erik had been skeptical about being able to enjoy the movie. But the darkness and theater-like sound pulled him into a flick that had plenty of jump scares, minimal plot, and absolutely no connection to reality.

The darkness, popcorn, and Ben's closeness helped Erik let go of more tension he didn't realize he still held. Ben didn't try to initiate anything, just snuggled, making Erik feel loved and cherished.

They finished the shark movie and started a lizard-monster flick Erik had put on their list. While they started off laughing at the special effects, the creature's rampage drew them in, and Erik found himself clutching Ben's hand, white-knuckled, by the explosive conclusion.

"Feel better?" Ben asked when the credits rolled.

"Surprisingly, yes," Erik admitted. "You're a miracle worker."

Ben snorted. "Hardly. I just figured we could feel good about not having to deal with a mega-shark or a radioactive lizard."

"At least as far as we know," Erik teased.

"Shh. Don't jinx us."

Erik shut off the television and sound system while Ben carried the popcorn bucket, soda cans, and beer bottles to the kitchen.

Once they were in bed, Erik turned to Ben. "What do you want?" He looked into Ben's eyes.

"You had the rough day. I should be asking you," Ben replied. "I'll take anything you'll give me. What would make you feel good?"

"Make love to me," Erik whispered. "I want to feel you and hold you and know I'm safe."

"I'll do whatever's necessary to keep you safe," Ben replied. "You know that."

Erik nodded. "And it scares me because I don't want you to get hurt."

"Same goes for you." Ben slid his hands over Erik's body, reaffirming his claim. "So we just have to watch out for each other."

Ben took his time, lavishing Erik's mouth and throat with attention before moving slowly down to his chest and nipples. Ben's hands and lips showed his appreciation to Erik's bare skin before dipping lower.

Before he ever reached for the lube, Ben sucked Erik's cock to hardness and licked at his balls and taint. He pushed Erik's thighs wide open and rimmed him until Erik begged for release.

"Gonna make this good." Ben slicked up his fingers and loosened Erik's clenched hole, angling to hit his spot over and over until Erik was writhing and humping himself on Ben's hand.

"Please," Erik moaned.

Ben moved into position and pushed inside, sinking slowly into Erik's tight channel until he was balls deep.

Erik locked his ankles behind Ben's back. "Move," he whispered.

Ben rocked in and out, slowly at first, setting up a rhythm. Erik tangled one fist in the sheets and reached for his cock with the other. "Yes. Please. More." Erik didn't seem to be able to manage full sentences.

"Gonna take good care of you." Ben picked up the pace.

Erik knew his partner could read everything in his eyes—love, lust, vulnerability, and the vestiges of the day's tension. He could see the same in Ben's gaze, along with an intensity that made him tremble.

He'd never trusted anyone like he did Ben, allowing him to see his fears and insecurities and the depths of his emotions. Erik had learned early to keep parts of himself hidden, to nest the tender places behind armor, and to take precautions to avoid having his feelings used against him. Ben managed to disarm his protections and prove himself worthy of Erik's faith, which only made Erik love him more.

Erik felt the urgency in Ben's thrusts, insistent but not rough, and sensed the tide of his orgasm rise as they moved together. Erik climaxed first, spurting over his fist and onto his belly. Ben came seconds later, working them both through the aftershocks before he leaned down and kissed Erik on the lips.

"Better?" Ben moved back far enough to meet Erik's gaze.

Sated and still riding the high, Erik nodded. "Definitely."

Ben pulled out carefully and padded to the bathroom, returning a few moments later with a warm, wet washcloth. "Let me," he said when Erik reached for it and wiped down Erik's belly and between his thighs, a gentle intimacy.

"Ready to sleep?" Ben tossed the washcloth away and settled down beneath the covers next to Erik.

Erik nodded. "Yeah. Barely keeping my eyes open. I think you used me up."

Ben chuckled. "I'll remind you of that in the morning. There's time for a second round before breakfast to start the day right."

Erik kissed Ben goodnight and closed his eyes, keeping his thoughts focused on the warmth of his lover's body, the smell of sex and their colognes, the softness of the linens around him.

Tonight he was loved and safe. Tomorrow would come soon enough.

———

The cold morning wind off the ocean made Erik shiver despite his coat and hat. He and Ben joined Alessia, her coven, and other volunteers to raise a protective barrier around the site where the Commodore Wilson once stood as the autumn equinox made the genius loci's power wax stronger.

The participants formed a circle around the empty lot. A little farther back, clearly an observer and not part of the ritual, Chief Hendricks sat warm and toasty inside his idling squad car.

Monty Clark nodded in acknowledgment as did Susan. Jaxon and Arjun came to stand next to Ben and Erik, looking equally cold despite their wool coats and scarves.

"At least it's not as cold as it was at the winter solstice last year."

Jaxon ran his mittened hands up and down his arms.

"Still too bloody cold," Arjun muttered.

"It's a short ritual." Erik tried to take that solace to heart.

"Yeah, it takes longer for hypothermia to set in," Ben snarked. Erik elbowed him in the ribs, and Ben pretended to be wounded.

Jaxon and Arjun laughed. "Be careful," Arjun warned, playfully wagging a finger. "You sound like an old married couple—like us!"

Erik froze, unsure how Ben would react. To his relief, Ben grinned. "You say the nicest things."

A steady stream of people joined the circle until they ringed the empty plot. Alessia had an iron brazier surrounded by a tempered glass enclosure that kept the wind at bay. She struck a small bronze gong to get the group's attention.

"Thank you for coming," she called out above the wind and the surf. "Please hold hands during the ritual and lend your energy to creating an effective barrier. You aren't required to say anything, but if you feel moved to do so, you can say in unison 'rise and contain' between the verses of the incantation."

"It's worse, being this close to the site," Jaxon said. Erik and Ben nodded. Arjun just shivered. Jaxon maintained that Arjun's spectacular intuition was in part supernatural, even if Arjun himself wasn't convinced.

"Feel it?" Erik asked Ben.

"Yeah. It's all jangly and out of tune," Ben replied. "Like a band playing off-key."

Erik nodded, although to him, the malignant energy of the genius loci felt like the scrape of claws across slate. It left him with no doubt this was a "bad place" on a primal level.

"Makes you wonder how people stayed here," Ben murmured.

"The hotel was a massive construction of stone with iron supports," Jaxon replied. "That probably tempered the eerie feeling, although it clearly didn't change the owners' luck."

The gong chimed again, and they fell silent as Alessia began the ritual and took hands to form a human chain.

She spoke the first part in Latin, adding dry ingredients to the fire that filled the air with the scent of cedar, sage, and clove. Smoke rose from the brazier and spread out across the site, adding another layer of purification.

"We bind you to this land," she said.

"Rise and contain," the volunteers responded, adding their energy to the protective curtain of power Alessia wove with her spell.

"You will not harm the people of this place."

"Rise and contain."

This time, Erik thought he could make out a faint sparkle in the air around the perimeter of the site, just inside the human line.

"You will not cause ill-will or negativity."

"Rise and contain."

Now Erik felt certain he saw a faint scrim pulsating in the darkness.

"By the power of the light, the goodwill of those gathered, and the magic of my ancestors, I bind, weaken, and constrain the dark energy of this site."

"Rise and contain."

The supernatural curtain now appeared as a translucent, coruscating dome that covered the entire site.

"So mote it be!" Alessia's voice rose with the completion of the spell. Erik felt a frisson of power as a tingle down his spine and sudden warmth where he held hands with Ben on one side and Jaxon on the other.

For just a second, the supernatural dome flared bright before winking out. Although the light faded, Erik felt the remaining energy, a protective seal that would temper the strongest period of the genius loci's waxing energy before its negative power returned to a low hum.

"The ritual is concluded. Thank you for your help."

Erik thought that Alessia looked spent from raising powerful magic, even with the help of the volunteers. He didn't consider his own abilities to be "magic" per se, although that definition was up for debate. But he knew that during difficult "reads" of objects with his psychometry he had borrowed energy from Ben and others linked by touch. Erik could only imagine how that would be scaled up with the contribution of the dozens of people tonight.

As he let go of Ben's hand and turned, Erik caught a glimpse of motion. Holden Carr stood on the outside of the circle, partially hidden by a stand of seagrass.

"Carr's over there!" Erik pointed. They took off running in his direction just as Hendricks must have spotted him as well. The police car's lights came on, and Hendricks drove toward where Carr had been seconds before.

Erik's breath puffed in the cold air, and his lungs burned, but he kept pace with Ben as they sprinted after the elusive man. Hendricks sped past them, but Carr quickly left the sidewalk and the road, darting between houses and through yards.

Hendricks stopped the car and gave chase on foot. Erik and Ben spread out, trying to cover more territory. Dogs barked and security lights flared to life.

Minutes later they lost sight of him. Carr was gone.

Erik rejoined Ben and Hendricks and shook his head. "I didn't see him." Ben cursed, agreeing. All of them were out of breath.

"He shouldn't have been able to get away like that," Hendricks muttered, clearly pissed off at losing their suspect. "It's almost like he—"

"Has a magical artifact helping him?" Erik supplied. "If the rumors we heard are true, then I suspect Carr wanted to power up his item before the ritual tamped down the site's power. He might have hung around to see what was going on, figuring we'd be too distracted to notice him."

"Whatever he did, it worked, dammit," Hendricks groused. "Stay out of trouble." He gave a warning look to Ben and Erik before he drove off. Erik figured the chief needed to vent his anger by snapping at someone since Carr slipped their grasp.

Ben and Erik walked back to the Commodore Wilson site, where a few stragglers were just leaving. Jaxon and Arjun had waited for them and hurried over.

"We thought we saw Carr, but lost him. He's a slippery bastard," Erik said.

"Always was," Jaxon agreed. "I don't know about you, but I'm hungry again. Let's go get second breakfast."

The four of them adjourned to The Spike, which offered hearty breakfasts as well as being a favorite place for lunch and dinner. Erik always enjoyed spending time with Jaxon and Arjun, although the couples' busy schedules often interfered with plans to get together. Between Jaxon's time on Broadway and Arjun's adventures in high-tech, they had plenty of entertaining tales to share.

Erik suspected that Arjun and Jaxon took the lead, spinning stories to lighten the load for him and Ben, given the current situation. He went with the flow, appreciating the chance for a light-hearted meal with good friends.

Afterward, Ben walked Erik back to Trinkets. "I'm going to the office; I'll just leave work early and be done sooner."

"Okay. Be careful—Carr's still out there, and he's not done yet," Erik warned as he entered the security code.

Ben kissed him. "You too. Keep the doors locked until your usual time. Carr's got more reason to be looking for you than for me."

"I will," Erik promised. "Text me later?"

"Count on it."

Erik stepped inside and, with a stomach full of tangled emotions, watched Ben walk away. He still felt strange after the ritual, as if the combined power of the group and the dark energy of the genius loci was discordant music barely in earshot. Knowing Carr was still in town worried him, both on his own account and for Ben's safety.

The whole sordid business was coming to a boil, and Erik couldn't shake the feeling that he and Ben needed to solve the mystery of Edwin's missing treasure before Carr beat them to it.

Time was running out.

NINE

BEN

Ben arrived at the rental real estate office before Jenny and started a pot of coffee. He eyed the boxes of Raines's personal effects that were stacked in an unused office, where they'd sit until the search for legitimate next-of-kin had been exhausted. Having the boxes nearby gave him the creeps, but he didn't like the idea of putting them in a storage unit where they would be more vulnerable to theft.

"What a mess," he muttered, waiting for the coffee to brew.

It took a moment for Ben to notice the strange skritching from the back of the office. He had turned off the security system since Jenny was due soon, and now he wondered if he should have waited.

Ben grabbed the gun from his desk drawer and advanced on the back door, clearing each room as he passed. He moved silently, staying low to get the drop on an intruder.

He caught a glimpse of a man in a dark stocking cap and jacket hunching by the back door to pick the lock and opened his mouth to shout a warning before firing. Before he could speak, a cold wind swept through the hallway, turning the air frigid. Furious screams nearly deafened him, and a plume of red smoke streaked past Ben, slamming against the back door and shaping itself into a spectral face twisted with rage at the intruder.

"Get out!" a voice shouted so loud it shook the window glass.

Ben stepped back, wide-eyed, heart pounding. His gun wouldn't protect him against what he guessed to be Tom Raines's furious spirit.

For a moment, Ben spotted Holden Carr's face through the window. Carr held up something long and slender, covered with gold, and shouted something Ben didn't understand.

Raines's ghost shrieked in torment and dissipated in long streaks of red mist as if the gold artifact had shredded his soul.

Ben raised his gun to fire, but Carr had vanished.

"Fuck!" Ben raced to the door and threw it open, but Carr was gone—or magically hidden from his sight. Venturing after him without being able to spot his target was asking for trouble. Cursing under his breath, Ben slammed the door behind him and turned the security system back on.

He leaned against the wall, letting the adrenaline crash. *What the fuck was up with that ghost?*

Ben hadn't sensed Tom Raines's spirit before this, but perhaps the old man had just been biding his time or needed to gather enough mojo to make himself seen.

Whatever Carr held up and shouted drained the energy right out of Raines. What scares a ghost?

Realizing that the spirit might not remain incapacitated for long and unwilling to have a show-down with a furious ghost, Ben hurried to the kitchen and grabbed salt. He went to the storage room and made a circle around the stack of boxes, pouring salt over top of them for good measure.

When he ran out, Ben set the canister aside and realized his hands were shaking. He didn't know what freaked him out more—Carr's attempted break-in and strange vanishing trick or the vengeful spirit.

The ghost. Definitely the ghost.

But whatever freaky thing Carr used to tear up the ghost was terrifying too.

Ben hurried to his office and cradled the cup in his hands as he waited for his heartbeat to slow to normal.

His phone rang, and he startled, spilling coffee on himself.

"Shit." He blotted the drips as he accepted the call.

"Hi, Teag. What do you have for me?" He hoped his voice sounded halfway normal.

"Plenty—I just hope it helps," Teag replied. "Is this a good time?"

"Yeah. I just got attacked by Raines's pissed-off ghost, but he's gone now." Ben realized how strange that sentence sounded after it was out of his mouth.

"Want to run that by me again?"

Ben told Teag about finding Carr's hideout with its occult trappings, the ritual that morning, chasing Carr, and then Carr's break-in attempt and the ghost's angry response.

"You guys don't do anything halfway up there, do you?" Teag replied. "I think I can shed light on how Carr got away from you so easily. He was using a magical relic, borrowing its power. With a genius loci so close and it being the equinox, he probably powered up before your witch friend contained the energy."

"So he's super-powered now?" Ben had thought the situation couldn't get any worse.

"Not really," Teag replied. "At least, not permanently. Carr got his magical battery all charged, but he won't be able to recharge with the ritual warding in place, so every time he uses his relic, it drains the juice. From what you've described, he's used it three times already. It won't last forever, and the waning energy now that the equinox has passed will drain his relic even faster."

"How did he make himself invisible?"

"He didn't," Teag said, chuckling. "It's a damn good distraction spell. Like those special ops uniforms that make people blend into their surroundings. 'Cryptic coloration' is the official name. The spell works in a similar way, taking your eye away from where he is and letting him fade into the background."

"I guess that's better than actual invisibility."

"It would take a powerful witch to pull that off, not just a hack with a relic," Teag assured him.

"Fill me in." Ben sipped his coffee.

"While we're still talking about this morning's excitement, that item you saw Carr hold up? The one that looked like a golden pencil? I'd bet good money it's a bone of Santa Romola Fiorella, patron of the New Jersey mafia," Teag said. "She's the saint you found the shrine to in his room. One of the miracles associated with her was hiding criminals from the police, even when the crooks should have been in plain sight."

"So the relic actually works?"

"For now," Teag said. "I suspect that Carr owes a big debt to a powerful witch, and maybe to clear his account he needs to deliver some of the missing heist money. The witch might have given him the relic to help him, but those kinds of magical items always have a cost to the user. Since his witch patron won't need him after he hands over the money, I suspect the relic will drain him when it can't leech off other sources."

"If he beats us to the treasure, at least he'll die happy," Ben muttered.

"So about that. Santa Romola was also known as a finder of lost things. Carr has stepped up his game by not just praying but using a— probably stolen—relic. That could work as a divining crystal to help him find a location on a map."

Ben had heard of witches and psychics using a crystal pendant suspended over a map to pinpoint a target, trusting the magic to pull the crystal over the right place. He could imagine substituting the gold-covered bone for the pointer, although the idea of possessing part of someone's skeleton gave him the heebie-jeebies.

"Ick. Does it really work?"

"According to the legends...maybe? There's certainly precedence with people making remarkable claims about other saints' relics," Teag replied.

"If Carr has the relic to help him find the treasure, then we're screwed. We still have no idea where to look other than 'the Pine Barrens.'"

"Not exactly." Teag's voice held a smile. "I think I cracked the code on the poker chips—with a little help from some friends on the Darke Web. The grouping of numbers looked right to be coordinates, but the numbers themselves didn't make any sense. So I looked for a substitution code. Those codes swap out one digit for another, according to a key. They're simple to make and can be challenging to break. Fortunately, I suspect Edwin was in a hurry. Once I cracked the code, it gave me coordinates that fit within the Pine Barrens. Check your inbox—I sent the info by encrypted email."

"Thank you." Ben felt like maybe, for once, they had an advantage again.

"Oh, and I did a little more digging into Tom Raines," Teag said. "He was very careful about guarding his self-imposed exile in Maine, but the few times he slipped up were enough to find him."

"How did he manage to hide so well all those years?" Ben wondered.

"He must have been working on his new identity for a while because it held up well," Teag replied. "He showed up in Maine as Fred Bowers and paid cash for a vacation cabin on one of the islands. Looks like he paid cash for most things, which probably was just fine with his neighbors.

"His stash tided him over for a long time. I suspect he did some under-the-table odd jobs to stretch his nest egg, but the past few years, he must have been running dry," Teag went on. "I found late notices on his utility bills, that sort of thing. Which would explain why he would risk leaving his safe haven to look for his grandfather's hidden money."

"He had a good run." Ben admired Raines's skill at hiding and staying hidden. "Too bad he couldn't just quietly fade away." Raines was a criminal, but Ben couldn't work up too much judgment over stealing from the Mob.

"I guess he gambled that no one was looking for him anymore," Teag said. "He lost the bet. I suspect that one of those mafia witches you asked about put some kind of spell on the area that would trigger if he came back, and that alerted the wrong people."

"What did you find out about a 'supernatural syndicate' and the Bone Men?"

Teag paused. "You really want to know? Once you do, you can't un-know it."

"If it's killing people in my rental units—literally on my doorstep— I don't really have a choice."

Teag sighed. "I'll give you the quick version, and we can talk about the details later. Yes, there are crime syndicates of supernatural beings —witches, vampires, werewolves, psychics, and some fae. Even the mobsters are scared—or exceptionally respectful—of them. The 'Bone Men' are witches with deep ties to the Mob who are allied with the different mafia families and syndicates but are actually self-interested when push comes to shove.

"The supernatural syndicates are involved in everything from shifter trafficking to creating and selling pharmaceuticals engineered to work with paranormal metabolisms—for medicine and recreation. They've got connections to money laundering—hiding long life spans and multiple identities—online fraud, relic theft, and artifact appro-priation, among other things."

"Which makes sense with some of the stuff Erik ran into," Ben mused.

"Exactly. We've clashed with elements of the syndicate and so have some of our hunter friends," Teag replied. "There are the usual internal rivalries like with the normal Mob—and their grudges can span centuries. The syndicates are a nasty piece of work, and the Bone Men are the worst of the worst. I liked it better when we thought the monsters worked solo."

"No kidding," Ben agreed. "Thanks for the update."

"Like I said, I can give you more details whenever you want or need them, but that gives you an idea of why Carr's back is against the wall. He's got nothing to lose. Be careful."

Ben thanked Teag and promised to stay in touch. When the call ended, he brought out a paper map of New Jersey and plotted the coordinates Teag supplied.

The remote spot fell between hiking trails and public areas, acces-sible but not where people were likely to find it by accident. For a desperate man with a limited chance to stash his money, Edwin had made a smart choice.

Assuming it's still there. If he buried a bunch of gold and silver and someone found it, it would be untraceable. The finder would just need a good cover story and a discreet person to fence it to. We could get there and it could be a bust.

Remind me again why this is our problem?

Unfair as it was, Edwin's heist became an issue for him and Erik when the poker chips showed up at Trinkets and Tom Raines died in the rental unit. Until the treasure was found, the factions involved would never believe Erik and Ben weren't involved. Carr's use of dark magic also meant regular law enforcement was at a deadly disadvantage, requiring specialized knowledge to handle the threat—the kind of knowledge and experience Erik and Ben had.

Somehow, we've become the guardians of Cape May—along with Monty, Alessia, and the others with abilities.

I guess that's not such a bad thing—or much different from being a cop. At least we've got friends who have our back.

Resigned, Ben reached for his phone and called Erik. "Teag's got coordinates for the Pine Barrens. We need a plan—and then it's time for a road trip."

Next, he reached out to Alessia. "We could really use your help." He explained the situation, including Carr's relic and borrowed magic—and the possibility of a pissed off Mob *strega*.

"Santa Romola? Wow—that's dark stuff," Alessia replied. "I'd warn you about crossing the 'supernatural syndicate,' but it's too late for that. Santa Romola has the most devotees among the Sicilian Mob—and you never want to cross them when magic or money is on the line."

"Can you help?" Ben didn't like dragging Alessia in deeper than she already was, but he didn't know what they'd be facing at the treasure site. He had no problem asking for backup.

"Of course. Get what you need for your part, and meet me at my shop. With luck, we'll have this sorted out by supper." Alessia sounded far more chipper than Ben felt.

Erik was ready by the time Ben arrived at their apartment. He wore jeans and work boots, with a T-shirt and flannel layered under a canvas jacket, along with a knit cap, scarf, and leather gloves.

"God, Erik. You look like you're ready for grave digging."

Erik shrugged. "Graves, treasure—not much difference. Get changed and grab your Glock. I've got shovels at the shop to put in the trunk. The bag has the poker chips, maps, bullets, some handy tools, and a medical kit, plus what I'll need to do wardings if it comes to that."

"Alessia is coming with us, so hopefully she can handle the heavy-duty magic," Ben said.

"Good. We're going to need the help."

Ben changed into his hiking clothes, including well-worn boots and a sturdy coat. Despite everything going on, Ben had to admit that the sight of Erik with a shoulder holster sent a jolt straight to his cock.

Then again, Erik seemed to appreciate Ben's thigh rig, so maybe they were on the same page.

Alessia came to meet them when they pulled up at the curb outside her store. Her black jeans, boots, turtleneck, and jacket held a defi-nitely witchy vibe—*or maybe, secret agent*, Ben thought. She carried a bulging duffel bag. Ben didn't see a weapon, but Alessia's magic might be all she needed.

"I've been thinking about what you told me," she said as she climbed into the backseat. "Teag does good research. I think it's inter-esting that Edwin Raines buried his treasure in the Pine Barrens. I wonder if he had a touch of magic himself."

"Why's that?" Erik turned slightly in his seat as Ben pulled away from the curb.

"The Barrens has plenty of mojo of its own—a neutral genius loci. Nature spirits aren't uncommon, but everything we've built up and how we change the land can make it difficult to sense them," she replied. "Places that have remained largely undeveloped or were chosen as national and state parks or preserves tend to have unusually strong genius loci that subconsciously sway their conservationists."

"I never thought about that, but it makes sense," Erik said. "They also tend to be places that inspire awe."

"Aside from natural beauty, that sense of transcendence is usually your hindbrain recognizing the area's nature spirit," Alessia said. "Since the Barrens don't have a reputation for having a malicious vibe, like the Commodore Wilson site, that works in our favor. The genius loci may sense the stain of the treasure buried there and be happy to have it removed."

"You think the land is that aware?" Ben had grown up seeing ghosts and hearing about people's nonnas who could cast the Evil Eye, but between Erik's abilities and their friends' supernatural gifts, there had been a sharp learning curve.

"Many people believe the land has always been conscious." Alessia settled into her seat. "We just don't listen to it. In the places where its voice is loudest, we either create a shrine or block it off as a danger. Those tend to be sites for strong magic as well."

"Do you think Edwin knew about the land spirit?" Erik asked.

"Probably not," Alessia replied. "He knew he was being watched, needed time to wrap up his affairs, and chose the best place he could think of where no one might find it. I suspect that, in a way, the Barrens' genius loci even shielded the treasure from people with ill intent. Folks have believed the Pine Barrens to be a place of natural power for a very long time."

During the drive, they planned how best to ward the area and protect themselves. Alessia had the spells already worked out. Erik and Ben decided to take turns digging so one of them could have a gun ready in case of unwanted company.

"Do you think Carr will get there before we do?" Erik asked as Ben drove, keeping just above the speed limit.

"If he used magic, it's a toss-up," Alessia said. "Depending on the spell and his skill casting it. Without the real coordinates, the relic's directions are likely to be approximate unless he's a very careful witch."

"I don't think Carr is a witch at all," Erik replied.

"Hmm. I think our odds are good that we might beat him to it, but no guarantee."

It took just under two hours to drive to the part of the Pine Barrens indicated by the coordinates and another half hour to hike from the parking area to the exact spot. The location looked untouched and completely unremarkable.

"Are you sure this is it?" Erik asked Ben and shifted the gear bag on his shoulder as he surveyed the area.

"If Teag's translation of the coordinates is right, I'm standing on top of the spot where we need to dig," Ben replied.

To Ben's relief, Carr was nowhere in sight.

Alessia took the items she needed out of her bag and immediately began to set down a salt circle large enough for the three of them and the hole they planned to dig.

"The Pine Barrens has its share of ghosts," she explained. "We don't need gawkers or interference. Most of them are *probably* harmless, but there are rumors about Mob victims and missing persons being dumped in the forest, so it's best not to take chances."

Next, she put down a long, woven cord around an area within the larger circle to create a warded workspace for her magic. She laid out candles and her chalice, taking precautions against starting a fire.

"Go ahead and start digging," she told them. "I'll set up protections and distraction spells. Let's hope we don't need them."

Erik stayed on watch while Ben set his coat aside and began to dig. The sandy soil threatened to fill in what he had just removed, but the moisture from a recent rain made the job a little easier.

"I hope he didn't bury it like a body," Ben said. "Six feet down is a deep hole."

"I doubt he had time." Erik scanned the horizon for threats. "He would have gone down far enough to protect it from animals, but he expected to return shortly."

Ben dragged his sleeve across his forehead. "I have new respect for gravediggers."

Alessia chanted. Erik remained a silent, protective presence with his gun drawn. Ben concentrated on the *shish-shish* of the sandy soil on the iron shovel blade, trying to keep a regular rhythm and wondering how sore he would be in the morning.

The air smelled of pine and incense. Despite the chill, sweat trickled down Ben's back beneath his shirt and made damp hair cling to his forehead.

Alessia's chant finished with an exclamation, and she threw her hands toward the sky. Ben felt a prickle like he had at the Commodore Wilson ritual, and when he squinted, he thought he saw tiny sparkles like dust motes in the air all around them.

"Someone's coming," Alessia said quietly.

Ben kept digging. Erik raised his gun as Alessia began another chant.

"Dig faster," Erik urged.

Ben bit back a retort and pushed the shovel in deep. If they were truly in the right spot, he hoped to hit pay dirt soon.

On the next stroke, the tip of the shovel thudded into something. Ben was a little over two feet down. He scooped more dirt away, revealing what appeared to be a battered old suitcase.

"Found it!"

"Get away from that! It's mine!" Holden Carr burst through the trees. He held a gun in one hand and the gold relic in the other.

A shot fired.

Erik dove to put himself between Ben and the protective scrim, returning fire and rolling away. Alessia shouted a word of power.

The incoming bullet glanced off the magical dome and went wide. Erik's shot went right through, but Carr threw himself to the side. Before they could exchange another volley, Alessia gestured, and an invisible force tore the gun from Carr's hand and threw it into the brush.

"You've got no right!" Carr screamed, furious. Ben bet that terror over leaving his witch debt unpaid stoked the other man's anger.

"Neither do you," Erik retorted, keeping himself between Carr and the others.

Carr leveled the relic like an athame and yelled something Ben didn't quite catch. A force buffeted Alessia's warding, and she shouted in a language Ben had never heard. The sparkling dome held, making the dueling magics a contest of wills.

"Fuck this." Erik fired again, catching Carr in the bicep. Carr howled in pain and lost his focus, breaking off the attack.

"Drop the relic, or I'll shoot again," Erik threatened.

A wild, half-mad grin lit Carr's features as he came to his knees, launching another strike with the saint's bone, making the dome flare with light. When Ben's eyes adjusted, Carr had found refuge behind a tree where he could keep up his barrage while avoiding Erik's shots.

"Give up!" Erik covered Ben as his partner worked to dislodge the suitcase from where roots had grown around it. "The cops know all about you. They're looking for you."

"I'm not scared of the cops."

Alessia held back the magical assault, but Ben knew they couldn't keep the standoff going indefinitely.

"But the witch you owe is another matter, isn't it?" Erik called back, and Ben knew his partner was trying to rattle their attacker. "What happens if you can't pay him back? Will he kill you quick or curse you slow?"

"Shut up!" The bone glowed brightly in Carr's grip, and Ben remembered what Teag said about the relic having its own price. He wondered if Erik's intent was to push Carr to drain himself because their attacker seemed heedless of the energy his object expended.

"Can you get that damned bone away from him?" Ben asked as he cut through the web of thin roots.

"Not and keep the scrim intact," Alessia hissed. "The relic has real power."

Erik fired again, hitting the tree where Carr hid and sending up a spray of splinters. Carr stumbled back, losing his concentration, and the intensity of the relic's assault wavered. It seemed to Erik that the glow around the saint's bone had grown fainter during the fight.

"You really think the guy you owe is going to let you live after he's got the money?" Erik taunted. "He'll kill you—if your relic doesn't do it first."

Ben bit back a cry of triumph as his shovel cut through the last of the roots. He chipped away dirt from the edges of the suitcase, revealing a handle. Ben tugged, hoping the old bag didn't disintegrate, but it remained firmly lodged. Lying flat on the ground to stay out of the line of fire, Ben continued working to free the treasure while Erik and Alessia held off Carr.

"What happens if I shoot the relic?" Erik pitched his voice so only Ben and Alessia could hear.

"Don't know. It could come back on you. I wouldn't try it," she managed as she kept up the magical barrier.

"Shit. I was afraid you'd say that."

Erik fired again, hitting Carr's forearm this time. Carr shrieked and dropped the relic, bleeding heavily.

Erik dodged across the barrier and tackled Carr, meeting little resistance now that their attacker had been disarmed and was losing blood.

"We should leave you out here to deal with the witch," Erik told Carr as he tied him with the man's belt.

"I'll give you some of the money," Carr begged, eyes wide with pain and fear. "Just please don't make me break my promise to the witch."

"Not my problem." Erik used Carr's scarf to wrap both bullet wounds as best he could.

"You don't think he'll know you have the money? He'll come after you," Carr threatened.

"And we'll deal."

Ben pulled the suitcase free, and Erik scooped up the relic with the shovel's iron blade.

"I've got a containment pouch," Alessia said after she let the warding fall. "We can't leave that damned thing out here."

She set the cloth bag on the ground, opened wide. It looked to Ben as if the fabric had silver threads and sigils in a variety of colors woven into it. Erik carefully deposited the relic and pulled the drawstrings.

Carr lay sobbing behind Erik, no longer trying to put up a fight. Erik circled the area, returning with Carr's gun, which he handled with a mitten.

"Let's get out of here."

Alessia closed the warding and offered her thanks to the nature spirit of the Barrens, then gathered her materials. Ben wrapped his belt around the suitcase so it didn't burst open on the hike to the car.

Erik hauled Carr to his feet. "I didn't shoot you in the leg because I didn't want to carry your ass out of here. We'll get you to a doctor soon enough."

Alessia stepped closer, and put a hand over each of Carr's wounds in turn, stanching the flow of blood. "They aren't completely healed, but he's not going to bleed out."

Erik kept his gun in hand as they started the trek to the parking lot. The woods seemed too quiet, and he couldn't shake the feeling that they were being watched.

He had never been to the Pine Barrens before and thought they might be beautiful under other circumstances, especially in summer. The wind swept through the branches, rustling the thick needles like the murmur of distant voices.

Erik caught a flicker of movement, and old training kicked in just as the crack of a rifle shot broke the stillness. Carr staggered as a fresh wound stained his chest.

"Down!" Erik dragged Carr with him and threw himself on top of their prisoner as Ben returned fire from behind a downed tree trunk. Alessia spoke an arcane command, and the protective dome appeared again just as the sniper fired a second time. His shot skewed off into the forest and thudded into a tree.

The *rat-tat-tat* of an automatic weapon made Ben and Alessia flatten themselves on the ground. Despite everything, the magical dome held, but Erik knew it couldn't last forever.

Three men emerged from the trees. Two held high-caliber handguns and one carried an assault rifle. Dressed in black with their lower faces covered, they looked like a hit squad.

Ben and Erik rose just far enough to return fire when they realized their attackers' shots weren't getting through. Their own bullets, however, fired right past the barrier. The angle was bad and fouled their aim, but Ben managed to graze one man in the leg. Erik's bullet went low, hitting a second man in the stomach instead of center mass. Alessia shrieked a spell, and the third man's jacket caught on fire, forcing him to drop and roll.

For a few seconds, Ben felt a surge of relief before four more men opened fire from the tree line.

"Shit," Ben muttered. Alessia closed her eyes and pushed both hands, palms out, toward the protective barrier. Ben saw the strain in her face, the tension in her jaw. She had grown pale from the exertion, and he knew she couldn't maintain the protection forever.

Bullets sprayed the dome. Whoever had sent the goons after Carr and the treasure clearly had no intention of taking prisoners. Ben and Erik returned fire, but the new attackers used the tree line as a shield, making it difficult to aim. Alessia's protective barrier flickered.

No treasure is worth dying for, Ben thought, fearing the worst.

"What the hell is that?" One of the hitmen stopped firing and pointed.

Ben tracked the motion and stared, wide-eyed, at a huge stag with massive, glowing antlers that sauntered out of nowhere to stand between them and the attackers.

The goons turned their guns on the stag but the bullets went right through the majestic animal without harm.

"Look." Ben pointed as thick fog rolled out from the forest, although the day had been clear. The temperature plummeted to freezing. Faces and forms appeared in the mist and the woods were filled with otherworldly wailing and the screams of damned souls.

The attackers ran for the trail, leaving their gut-shot companion behind even as he called out to them and tried to crawl away.

The ghostly fog surged forward, skirting the luminous stag and the glowing dome. It swept over the wounded hitman, and he cried in terror as he disappeared in the depths of the fog and then went silent.

Relentless, the roiling fog pursued the men, who paused long enough to fire into it with no effect. Then the dark cloud overtook them, stifling their curses and panicked pleading.

Seconds later, the fog was gone as if it had never existed. Seven corpses lay on the ground, their faces frozen in fear, limbs twisted at unnatural angles.

The stag turned slowly and regarded them with ancient, dark eyes. Then he inclined his head in acknowledgment and walked with stately grandeur toward the trees, vanishing before he reached the darkness beneath the boughs.

"What did we just see?" Ben wasn't sure he trusted his voice.

"I have no idea," Erik said, looking completely stunned.

"The avatar of the forest's genius loci." Awe clear in Alessia's voice. "He saved us—along with the ghosts of the Pine Barrens."

"Did you call them?" Ben looked at their witch friend as if seeing her for the first time.

"Not exactly," Alessia replied. "I...made a plea to the spirit of the forest for help. And it answered. I guess it didn't like hitmen and stolen loot on its lands."

"I'm glad someone was listening." Erik sounded shaken. He rolled to one side, off of Carr's bloody form.

"Is he—" Ben asked.

Erik checked for a pulse. "Gone."

"Are you hurt? You're covered in blood."

Erik looked down at himself and shook his head. "None of it's mine."

Ben took charge. "Fuck. We've got to get out of here before someone reports all the noise. This does *not* look good, and we've got guns and a stolen treasure."

They took the suitcase and weapons, left the bodies where they lay, and hurried to the car, hoping not to run into any hikers. Ben drove carefully, minding the speed limit. Erik removed his bloodstained coat and did his best to wipe away the spatter on his face and hands. Alessia fell asleep in the back seat as soon as they pulled out of the lot.

"What the fuck do we do now?" Erik asked.

"Turn the money over to Hendricks, tell him that we managed to escape a fight between mobster gangs, and hope the Mob doesn't send more hitmen after us," Ben said. "It should be pretty clear from the crime scene that we were outnumbered."

"They're going to wonder how the hell we got out alive."

"Pretty sure Alessia can help come up with a cover story," Ben replied.

They were quiet for several miles. "You saw that stag, right? I didn't imagine it?" Erik asked.

Ben never took his eyes off the road. "I saw it. And the ghost cloud or whatever that was."

"Okay," Erik replied quietly. "Good. At least if I've gone nuts, we're both crazy."

They called Chief Hendricks at the edge of town and arranged to meet him in the parking lot of an abandoned warehouse. He rolled up in an unmarked vehicle, alone as they had requested. Ben, Erik, and Alessia stood next to their car, and Ben knew they all looked worse for the wear.

"What in the name of God happened to you?" Hendricks asked when he got out.

"We found Edwin Raines's long-lost treasure." Ben gestured toward the suitcase, which sat in front of their car on the ground. "He buried it in the Pine Barrens."

They had decided not to mention the glowing stag or the ghost protectors and told the chief that Carr and the Mob showed up while they were retrieving the suitcase but that Ben and the others had managed to sneak away during the battle.

Hendricks eyed the three of them, clearly suspecting there was more to the story. "Anything else you want to tell me?"

"No, sir," Erik said. If any of the bullets were matched to their registered guns, they'd deal with the issue then.

Hendrick's gaze raked over him, taking in the blood stains Erik hadn't been able to wipe away.

"How'd you find it?" he asked.

"Edwin Raines left coded directions on the poker chips that Dolores Quinn sent to Erik's shop. The chips were from the Fun Factory, the casino Edwin stole from," Ben said.

"Why am I hearing about these chips for the first time?" Hendricks demanded.

"We didn't know if they meant anything," Erik replied. "Technically, they weren't related to Tom's death. Edwin's theft wasn't being investigated."

Hendricks looked like he was grinding his teeth. Then he let out a breath and closed his eyes for a second before he shook his head. "I'll let that go…for now. What's in the suitcase?"

"Don't know," Ben said. "Didn't open it. But it's heavy as hell, so my guess is gold and silver, unless it's a bunch of rocks, and we've all gone to a lot of trouble for nothing."

"I'd suggest making sure there's a very public announcement about the lost heist money being turned over to the feds to keep any problems from following Ben and Erik," Alessia spoke up. Her voice sounded particularly honeyed, and Ben wondered if she might be nudging the cop with a bit of magic to cut them a break.

"Yeah, sure," Hendricks agreed. "Although I doubt that's the last we'll see of the Mob with the two of you in town." He glanced at Ben and Erik.

"On the other hand, they solved a decades-old cold case," Alessia said persuasively. "Recovered the stolen money and solved Dolores Quinn's attack."

Hendricks gave her a look. "Come again?"

"Her mother's ghost was attached to the poker chips, which had been hidden in their house," Erik replied. "She witnessed the attack by Holden Carr. He was looking for the chips and got angry when Dolores refused to turn them over."

"And you're just telling me this now?"

"It's been a bit busy," Erik said with a conciliatory half-smile.

"Speaking of Carr, any idea where he is now?" Hendricks glared at them suspiciously.

"Like we explained, he followed us to the Pine Barrens and got into a shootout with the guys who followed him. He's probably dead," Ben replied.

Hendricks passed a hand over his face. "And you left him there?"

"Cause we could have explained ourselves real easily to a bunch of unfamiliar police standing there with a dead guy and a suitcase of stolen gold. We thought we were doing well to get out when we did," Ben said dryly.

"Okay…" Hendricks wiped a hand over his mouth as he thought. "Give me a minute to figure out how to spin this. Just—don't leave town."

That he hadn't asked why Alessia was with them made Ben suspect that Hendricks knew the witch's reputation and believed in it.

Hendricks took the suitcase and left. Ben and the others got back into the car. "Well, that went better than it could have."

"Because we're not in a prison bus on the way to a Supermax?" Erik snarked.

"For starters, yes."

"I don't think you'll have any problems." Alessia gave a knowing smile. "The chief is very…receptive…to good ideas."

Ben knew Alessia's ethics didn't let her toy with people's minds, but he suspected that giving someone a nudge in the right direction skirted the rules.

"Thank you. I look terrible in orange." Erik looked to Ben. "I don't know about you, but I'm exhausted. Let's go home."

TEN
ERIK

Two weeks later

"**N**ow *this* is a vacation." Erik sank deeper in the steaming hot tub until the lavender-scented water lapped his chin. Ben sat beside him, enjoying the view from the climate-controlled conservatory that housed the tub.

"No argument on that from me," Ben replied, sounding equally relaxed.

The historic bed and breakfast was blissfully ghost-free, and Erik hadn't picked up any negative resonance from its antique furnishings. The food was as good as reviews bragged, and the location made it convenient to walk to shops and attractions.

"I've lived in New Jersey all my life and I'd never been to Point Pleasant before," Ben said. "Guess I was missing out."

"My parents had friends who raved about vacationing here. I came once a long time ago and liked it, so I was overdue for returning."

"What have you liked best?" Ben asked. For now, they were alone in the hot tub, but since privacy couldn't be guaranteed, they both

179

wore swim trunks. Ben had promised a more intimate encore in the large soaking tub in their bathroom.

"Hmm." Erik let the jets massage his back. Ben laid a hand on his thigh.

"Besides *that?*" Erik covered Ben's hand with his own. "All of it. The mini-golf was fun without the summer crowds. I enjoyed the aquarium and the boardwalk. I'm looking forward to the riverboat dinner cruise tomorrow night. And it was nice to just walk a different beach for a change. How about you?"

Ben leaned in to kiss him on the cheek. "All of that. Being away from the shop and the rental office for a break. And I seriously want to find out what brand of linens this place uses because they're awesome!"

"Maybe we can come back here next year," Ben said. "Make it an anniversary tradition."

Erik's breath caught at the implication of a future together.

Ben's eyes went wide as he seemed to realize what he had said, and for a moment, he had a deer-in-the-headlights look as if he might have said too much.

"I'd like that," Erik said quietly. "Anniversaries. Lots of them. With you."

He felt giddy and terrified at the possibility, and his stomach swooped like he was on a rollercoaster, but the essential rightness gave him courage.

"I'd like that too," Ben replied in a whisper, just before he met Erik halfway in a kiss.

Chief Hendricks had cleared them to leave town fairly quickly after the shootout at the Pine Barrens. Alessia and Monty teamed up to banish Tom Raines's ghost and do an in-depth magical cleansing of his rental unit to get rid of the last traces of his death. The feds took Edwin's treasure of gold bars and silver coins, accepting Hendrick's story that it had been found by anonymous hikers.

The skeletal remains of eight men were found in the Pine Barrens, picked clean by scavengers. Carr's bones were identified, and the other men proved to be known associates of crime families in Atlantic

City. No shell casings were found. The deaths were officially chalked up to a private Mob war.

The last Susan heard, Dolores Quinn was expected to make a full recovery from her injuries.

"I'd really love it if we could have a nice, quiet autumn," Erik replied. "It's probably too much to ask, but I can dream."

"We'll make it work," Ben assured him. "And for the record, I love living together. I hope you haven't had any regrets."

Erik squeezed his hand. "None at all. It's gone more smoothly than I expected. Feels like you've always been there." *And I hope that you'll always be there.*

He suspected the easy transition came from both of them making an extra effort, not wanting to relive any mistakes from the past. Whatever the reason, Erik wasn't going to second-guess the decision.

"Yeah," Ben agreed. "I love how comfortable it feels just being together." He gave Erik an exaggerated lustful grin. "As well as the hot sex."

They'd had a few tiffs, usually over where to store something or reconciling assumptions about cleaning routines. Erik was grateful that at this point in their lives, they had learned to "use their words" and recognize when unspoken expectations got in their way. Promising never to go to bed angry also kept little annoyances from spiraling into larger resentments.

"The hot sex is pretty awesome." Erik dared to brush his hand over Ben's crotch since there was no one currently nearby to see.

"Mostly, I just like waking up every day and you're there," Ben admitted. "We just...fit. I don't have to pretend to be someone I'm not. I can relax and be myself, and it's okay."

Erik smiled. "That's one of my favorite parts. I'm not walking on eggshells. I didn't even realize that I had been the last time until later. This feels right."

Ben took his hand. "I think so too."

Much as he loved the hot tub, Erik felt himself starting to prune. "I guess we should go back to the room," he said reluctantly.

"I guess. But we've got prosecco and a cheese tray waiting," Ben pointed out.

"I think they put chocolates on the pillows here," Erik agreed.

"Just the thing to go with strawberry lube," Ben whispered in his ear.

Erik grinned. "Good thing the night's still young."

AFTERWORD

I love to weave in real locations and history, as well as twist reality a bit to create places that are loosely based on fact. The Commodore Wilson hotel is inspired by the old Christian Admiral, which also had spectacular bad luck and a checkered past. The Fun Factory casino and entertainment complex really did exist in the early 1900s. The Pine Barrens are real and are said to be home to several legendary monsters, but as far as I know, no hidden treasure.

Santa Romola is a figment of my imagination, but the concept of saints venerated by mobsters and drug lords is real. If the supernatural syndicate reminds you of the witch disciples from the Witchbane series, there's a reason for that. And of course, Teag, Sorren, Chuck, and Robert Pettis figure prominently in the Deadly Curiosities series written under my Gail Z. Martin name. Ben didn't end up needing a favor from Vic D'Amato, but you can find Vic and his partner Simon in my Badlands series.

Thanks for reading!

ACKNOWLEDGMENTS

Thank you so much to my editor, Jean Rabe, to my husband and writing partner, Larry N. Martin, for all his behind-the-scenes hard work, to my beta readers, and my wonderful cover artist Lou Harper. Thanks also to the Shadow Alliance and the Worlds of Morgan Brice reader street teams for their support and encouragement, plus my promotional crew and the ever-growing legion of ARC readers who help spread the word!

I couldn't do it without you! And, of course, thanks and love to my "convention gang" of fellow authors for making road trips and virtual cons fun.

ABOUT THE AUTHOR

Morgan Brice is the romance pen name of bestselling author Gail Z. Martin. Morgan writes urban fantasy male/male paranormal romance, with plenty of action, adventure, and supernatural thrills to go with the happily ever after.

Gail writes epic fantasy and urban fantasy, and together with co-author hubby Larry N. Martin, steampunk and comedic horror, all of which have less romance and more explosions.

On the rare occasions Morgan isn't writing, she's either reading, cooking, or spoiling two very pampered dogs.

Watch for additional new series from Morgan Brice and more books in the Witchbane, Badlands, Treasure Trail, Kings of the Mountain, Sharps & Springfield, and Fox Hollow universes coming soon!

Where to find me, and how to stay in touch

Join my Worlds of Morgan Brice Facebook Group and get in on all the behind-the-scenes fun! My free reader group is the first to see cover reveals, learn tidbits about works-in-progress, have fun with exclusive contests and giveaways, find out about in-person get-togethers, and more! It's also where I find my beta readers, ARC readers, and launch team! Come join the party! https://www.Facebook.com/groups/WorldsOfMorganBrice

Find me on the web at https://morganbrice.com. You can also find me on Twitter: @MorganBriceBook, on Pinterest (for Morgan and Gail): pinterest.com/Gzmartin, on Instagram as MorganBriceAuthor, on YouTube at https://www.youtube.com/c/GailZMartinAuthor/ on

Bookbub https://www.bookbub.com/authors/morgan-brice and now on TikTok @MorganBriceAuthor

Check out the ongoing, online convention ConTinual www.facebook.com/groups/ConTinual

Support Indie Authors

When you support independent authors, you help influence what kind of books you'll see and what types of stories will be available because the authors themselves decide what to write, not a big publishing conglomerate. Independent authors are local creators supporting their families with the books they produce. Thank you for supporting independent authors and small press fiction!

ALSO BY MORGAN BRICE

Badlands Series

Badlands

Restless Nights, a Badlands Short Story

Lucky Town, a Badlands Novella

The Rising

Cover Me, a Badlands Short Story

Loose Ends

Leap of Faith, A Badlands/Witchbane Novella

Night, a Badlands Short Story

No Surrender

Warm You Up, a Badlands Short Story

Point Blank

Memory and Malice, a Badlands Novella

Shine Tonight, a Badlands Short Story

Fox Hollow Zodiac Series

Huntsman

Again

Fox Hollow Universe

Romp

Nutty for You

Imaginary Lover

Haven

Gruff

Trash and Treasure

Kings of the Mountain Series

Kings of the Mountain

The Christmas Spirit, a Kings of the Mountain Short Story

Sins of the Fathers

Kings of the Mountain Universe

Roustabout

Sharps & Springfield Series

Peacemaker

Treasure Trail Series

Treasure Trail

Blink

Last Resort

Secrets and Ciphers, a Treasure Trail Novella

Treasure Trail Universe

Light My Way Home, a Treasure Trail Short Story

Witchbane Series

Witchbane

Burn, a Witchbane Novella

Dark Rivers

Flame and Ash

Unholy

The Devil You Know

Signs and Wonders

The Christmas Crunch, a Witchbane Short Story

Sandwiched, a Witchbane Short Story

Ambushed, A Witchbane Novella

www.ingramcontent.com/pod-product-compliance
Lightning Source LLC
Chambersburg PA
CBHW030428120726
47903CB00003B/862